Meet Me In Atlantis

By Megan Sebastian

Second Edition, March 2013

Copyright © 2012 by Megan Sebastian

All rights reserved.

Table of Contents

DAY 1   4:16 P.M. 5

DAY 2   5:12 A.M. 10

DAY 3   6:38 A.M. 18

DAY 4   7:39 A.M. 26

DAY 5   7:56 A.M. 41

DAY 6   4:32 A.M. 53

DAY 7 6:42 A.M. 71

DAY 8   5:46 A.M. 87

DAY 9   5:45 A.M. 118

DAY 10 4:35 A.M. 135

DAY 11 4:46 A.M. 149

DAY 12 4:36 A.M. 175

DAY 13 4:14 A.M. 188

DAY 14 8:44 A.M. 206

For Paul

It actually happened. The end of the world as we know it has been caused by a geomagnetic reversal. The North Pole is now the South Pole and the South Pole is now the North Pole.

I had been hunkered under this table for three days, with the Earth rumbling almost constantly when I began to feel an odd pulling sensation. It felt almost like the force you feel when riding a merry-go-round. That lasted about five minutes, slowly building in strength and force, and then came a sudden jerk where everything slid hard right. At the same time, there came a huge, loud boom --- like a sonic boom, but louder and far more terrifying.

It has been about six hours since the boom, and it almost seems as if that were the culmination. The poles have reversed and things might be settling down now. The constant rumbling has stopped and the gusts of wind don't seem to be as frequent. For the past three days, the wind howled nonstop, the rain came down in sheets and earthquakes seemed to increase in number and intensity right before the pull. I heard cracking and crashes, like trees and utility poles and who knows what else coming down and breaking up out there. I thought I heard screaming down the street and maybe even a gunshot.

I don't know if this is the completion of the reversal or how I would know if something else is coming. I have been paralyzed with fear for the past three days, so at least the pull and the boom has spurred me to action and driven me to pull out this journal and find a pen and begin to write down what has happened so I can try to maintain a thread of sanity.

Across the world, people knew something big was starting to happen, but I don't think I or anyone could have imagined how the Earth could actually pitch and shake and feel as though it is splitting apart at the seams. It began several months ago with an escalation of extreme weather, and then satellites and electronic devices started getting a little wonky. The interruptions in service to the phones, televisions, Internet and handhelds began to spike and last for longer and longer spans of time. Natural disasters and odd weather patterns took a steep climb, and the experts finally started to agree this might be out of the ordinary and might be caused by an upcoming geomagnetic reversal. That was about the last thing they agreed on.

Geomagnetic reversal has happened several times on the planet, but the last time it happened was more than seven hundred thousand years ago. Some scientists said it would not be physical, that what we were experiencing would be the worst of it, like an old house settling on its foundation. Some predicted destruction on such a mass scale that nothing would survive. And there was every opinion in between the two extremes. I wish I had listened a little more closely to those extremists. No one ever does.

Three days ago, a sudden surge of natural disasters across the world began happening, each within hours of one another. The New Madrid fault started producing massive earthquakes, a tsunami hit Seattle and a volcano in Yellowstone blew up. Events were coming too fast and furiously worldwide to be reported by the media. Earthquakes were felt all over the world, large ones on all faults on every continent, and even small ones here in Denver. That day took everyone by surprise, and the newscasters let us know to take cover. News communication would be ending shortly as everyone scrambled for safety because things were going to get even rougher.

The poles had begun the migration in earnest. The magnetization was exerting serious disruptions on gravity. Electronics -- and all power -- would soon completely shut down as the reversal speeded up. No one could say how long something like this might last or what might be involved.

I knew I had to do something. Having no idea how to prepare for a great catastrophe, I pulled my huge dining table across the kitchen and pushed it against the back door, barricaded it with mattresses, grabbed as many essential supplies as I could find that I felt I might need at the end of the world and crawled underneath. The back door has a large dog door that leads to the backyard; in a worst-case scenario I can use it as an escape hatch.

I am still in shock that the planet has undergone what was clearly the end of the world as we know it and I am hunkered alone under my dining table, writing about it in a journal.

Day 1   4:16 p.m.

Not that you can tell night from day since the bang, but I have to start documenting and chronicling for myself, so I will call this Day 1.

It has been nineteen hours since the boom, and I have been under this table now for a total of four days, alternately bawling my eyes out and frantically praying and planning. There has been semi darkness with a good rain falling, but maybe showing signs of lightening. The rumbling has stopped and the wind seems to have quieted, with a few gusts here and there, but nothing like it was before the pull and the bang which hopefully indicated that the reversal was complete.

I secured the house pretty well before it fell down around me, but I should not have wasted the time because I have not been able to push the mattresses I originally propped against the table outward so it is probably in shambles.

I am eternally grateful for the antique French farmhouse table Mark had to have. Sturdy enough to have lasted a couple hundred years, it seems also to have been able to withstand the second floor of the house crashing down on it. The twelve- by four-foot space has become my world, and my emergency backpack and small stockpile of supplies has become my security. I guess I have to count my gun and two boxes of bullets in there as security too.

I hope this is going to be one of those "solidarity during times of strife" type events, but I can't count on that. The neighborhood seems eerily quiet at this point. On the day of the upheaval it seemed as though a lot of people were leaving and running around to try and get to where they felt safe or go to be with family so they could face whatever was coming together, so I don't know who is left on my street or in the neighborhood.

Why, oh why, did I not go when I had the ... No, I can't think like that. I did not. Getting my hands on the trial medication for my patient was my priority that day. I'm glad that I did get it to her. I gave her the entire enormous amount, too, in light of what was happening, so if she survived this she will be happy and comfortable and have a chance for long-term recovery. So I am glad for that. I'm also glad I did not strike out that afternoon when the world started to crack apart. Judging from what was happening around here, I would not have done well, exposed out in the open.

I just can't believe the unthinkable has happened and I have been separated from my family at a time like this. Mark left early the morning the worst of the disaster began to strike and made it up to our cabin in South Park with the twins, but I waited too long and here I am under the table. It was actually the cat and dog that alerted him that something big was about to happen that day. Early in the morning, before the world broke apart, they could not stop pacing back and forth, which is very out of character for them. They are both so old that the only time they usually got up was to eat or follow a sunbeam across the room for a better nap experience, but on that day they could not relax and lie down. Mark took their cue that something big was on the way that they could sense in the air and humans could not. He packed up fast and headed out with the family to our cabin in the mountains long before everyone else turned on the news to see the chaos beginning. I was supposed to be meeting them within a few hours, but the catastrophe was much bigger than I or anyone thought would overtake us so quickly.

He called me when he arrived, so I know they made it and I presume all still are safe. The cabin was our disaster plan, and it has been prepared for almost any eventuality, so I am positive they weathered the storm up there.

I wonder what is happening in other countries. Millions hunkered down like me? I wonder how many people actually survived. I am hoping all the nice, normal people made it. This sort of catastrophe is on a scale that has never been seen. I just don't see how many could have lived through it. Although here I am, not a scratch on me.

I guess I will take stock of my backpack again. I'm so glad I packed the old frame trekking pack. It is large enough that I have all sorts of usable things in there, a variety of items that I think I might need for several days at least. Once I have everything I need well arranged in the backpack, what do I do? I didn't think I could be this scared, but I am beginning to realize this is not going to be a scenario that has rescuers.

I have a plan of sorts forming in my head. It seems as if things have settled enough that I can try to walk down the main street closest to my house and toward the Capitol. That's where the main governmental buildings are, the heart of downtown. I will see if any government entities have survived and see what kind of organization will have formed. I have not decided yet whether I will identify myself as a doctor or involve myself in that capacity. I have debated this in my head over and over. I just don't know what I am going to find when I get out there. I will of course help anyone I find in need. What I don't want is to be pressed into unending service and kept from my goal of getting to my family.

I don't know what I am going to find when I crawl out of my little hobo camp, but knowing Mark and the twins are safe is my personal relief.

In retrospect, I am glad we spent so much time up in South Park at the cabin, reinforcing things and making it a safe haven. We even dug out the old root cellar and had a company come in and make it into a bunker. Except they don't call it a bunker anymore, it is referred to as a reinforced room or safe room. We thought we were being a bit extremist, but the weird weather activity across the world really was making us nervous. Then we were talking to our neighbors out there who live there year round and have been working on their place for years. They have a large, amazing house which runs completely on wind and solar power. They showed us their safe room, and we almost fell over. I could have lived comfortably in their reinforced room any time, let alone at the end of the world. They are incredibly well set up for at least fifty years.

Our little room is pretty well stocked. I'll bet Mark will wish he stocked it with lots more toys. Or, knowing Mark, he will be teaching the kids to read or write or paint or something constructive.

I am so lucky to have him and those twins. It felt like I hit paydirt with him, and then they came along to sweeten the deal. We have been having so much fun and now this. Laugh. Oh, a little displaced petulance. I felt normal there for one millisecond.

We did have the perfect life happening, Mark and me. I know I am not idealizing or glossing just because the world as we know it has ended. He and I have always had such fun together. We don't fight. We get irritated with one another, of course, but both of us are smart enough not to let small irritations build. I think both of us learned in previous relationships to just let a lot go. In any relationship, I am sure both partners feel they are giving one hundred ten percent and receiving only seventy. Mark has all the traits I love. He is tall, handsome smart and really funny. Non-judgmental. Easygoing. A good travel partner, which is very hard to find. We find endless things to talk about.

I miss them so badly, and I feel so horribly alone. I am going to have to turn off my headlamp and cry again. I know this is very self-serving, and I don't plan on being a walking disaster once I hit the streets, but for now I think it is cathartic.

Nights are hard because I can barely sleep. I have this bottle of old scotch in the emergency stash, but I am so scared to lose one iota of clarity or physical response time in case I need to react that I don't dare take a sip. I don't know that the physical destruction won't start back up again, and I can't be drunk if it does.

Day 2 5:12 a.m.

Today is the day. I must make some sort of move. I cannot spend one more day or night under this table. I have not been brave enough to do more than open the dog door and check to see what is going on outside. I need to know it is morning when I do that, for some primal reason.

The aftershocks seem to have passed. There is now a light rain, and gusts of wind here and there. Hopefully anything that was unstable has fallen by now. It should be safe enough to go out into the backyard and take a look around. If it feels OK I will grab my pack and head out. I have checked through my backpack more than a hundred times, it seems, and I have a lot of great stuff, but it is hard to know what I will need out there in the short and long term. I wonder if there are people stirring about, or is it the wind? Maybe it is more like I feel energy moving about out there.

It is going to be tough to do this alone. I am thrilled to be unhurt physically. I feel that I have everything I will need for my journey to South Park. I have the skills and wiles, sturdy waterproof hiking boots, plenty of freeze-dried food and a head-to-toe rain poncho. I have my light backpacking tent, batteries for my head lamp and many other small items too numerous to mention but that feel essential. I am not sure what I am going to face but I must remind myself that life is but a dream -- backed up by my gun, of course.

A little goal of mine is to get to South Park in a week. It may be unrealistic but it helps to have something in mind to displace the abject terror. It also helps to hold a picture of Mark and the babies in my head. I know Mark must be beside himself with worry for me. His last words to me were, "Make sure you meet me at the cabin."

8:20 a.m.

I am in complete and utter shock. I could barely make it through the dog door and into the rubble of what was once the backyard. I had always loved the fact that we lived in an older neighborhood with a lot of character and mature trees, but on the ground the trees seem so huge and their branches and their wood is everywhere and hard to climb over and through. The house is collapsed under huge trees, a telephone pole and all kinds of debris. I made it to our street, where every house has major damage. Most are collapsed under trees and poles like ours. Imploded buildings, trees and branches down everywhere, utility poles fallen over with power lines draped hither and thither, fences, rocks, glass, cars everywhere. It is complete destruction. I could not see the ground for the rubble. The pavement, streets and sidewalks are buckled and peeled back and missing in spots, exposing all the pipes and sewer and I don't know what. There is a rushing torrent of water under one part of an exposed sidewalk across the street. Cars are scattered and upended from the buckling and heaving, and that adds to the piles. On the main street, the damage looks even worse, like something I would see in a movie or like the footage I've seen on the news about a faraway war zone.

I saw two other people but made sure they did not see me. I am not ready and they did not look like the kind of folks I want to throw my lot in with anyway. One was a man pulling a little red wagon loaded down and covered with a blanket. Frankly, he looked a bit crazy. There was a person in a black trench coat and hat standing about three blocks down with his or her back to me, looking intently into the distance. I know I will look a little odd in all my clothes and gear, topped by a big poncho to block the rain, but that person was somehow giving off a sinister vibe. I don't know if, like a trapped or injured animal, I am on some sort of super-high alert and my body is secreting a chemical laced with adrenaline, or if the energy feels lighter, easier to read somehow. Every nerve of my being feels tuned to a fine frequency.

I ducked back before he or she might turn, and figured it was time to head back and regroup.

Exhale of long, deep breath. I am digging out that bottle of scotch because I need a big belt of it right now. I have never been so glad to be a responsible gun owner who has practiced with her firearm. I felt vulnerable out there. I was not feeling that great to start with because, as I was crawling out through the dog door, a light went off in my head that said you'd better try and see if that pack will fit out behind you, and of course the frame is just a little too big. I thought, well, I will just take some things out here and there and try to squeeze it through, and then I almost had it through when it bent and broke in two places. When I put it on and tried to get the bottom belt and straps to fit, a piece of the frame started poking me so I had to readjust and then use one of those stretch cords just to keep it in place on my back so I could hold the gun at ready in my hand. Now the whole get-up feels jerry-rigged to my body, and not stable at all. I had to leave the pack outside in the remains of the backyard when I went exploring so I could be light on my feet and then again when I came back inside just now to write and compose myself and get some more clothes on. I will have to get more weight out of my newly busted-up backpack, so now I feel like I have just enough time to write and throw down some more scotch and mentally gird myself to just go.

I think the two miles downtown to the Capitol is going to be a wearying, dangerous trek. The amounts of rubble are amazing. Who and what is under there? What is going to happen if I fall and hurt myself? I need to stop writing and thinking and just go.

4:38 p.m.

What a day, what a day. I'm settled and I'm safe. I am incredibly tired and incredibly wired. I am going to try and write briefly to describe what happened and what I have found.

I made it down Colfax to the now ruin of the Capitol building. There is a small mobilization and tent encampment set up at Civic Center, across from the Capitol. It took all morning to carefully navigate the rubble and hide from anyone I saw. I did not want to be distracted from my goal. I saw one other mobilization of sorts set up at a church. There don't seem to be a lot of people out and about, and no army or military or police. I don't know if most people are remaining hunkered down or if there are not many survivors.

I pitched my tent at the park, which has been cleared of debris. There is a small band of people here who seem to be in the same situation as me -- either waiting for someone or getting ready to head out to try to make it somewhere. They all seemed as normal as one can seem in these circumstances. We are all layered in lots of clothing because it is cold. The light rain means you have to have a good outer layer because that incessant rain can really get into the cracks and crevices, so everyone is bundled past clear recognition. Most everyone has some sort of pack or conveyance for their things. Most people, like me, have a gun. Good ol' America. The oddest part is seeing the children. They are past being scared and see this as a fun change. They play and laugh and run around.

The only horrible encounter I had was with a dead body in a car. It was on a side street and the car was parked outside a destroyed house. The car had some power lines across it but otherwise was undamaged -- just parked right at the curb on an unbuckled part of pavement. I could see someone sitting upright in the driver's seat. There was no movement, so I had to go over and check it out and see if the person needed assistance. As I got closer and peered in, it was clear it was a woman and she was dead of what looked like a heart attack. Her seat was reclined slightly back and she was staring straight ahead with her right hand clenched around her upper left arm. I almost lost it thinking of all the people who are out there, hurt or injured and dying under the rubble with no one coming to help them out. I can't even imagine the amount of bodies a catastrophe of this magnitude could produce. Then the horrible me was glad she was already gone and I could move along.

I reached a point on Colfax where I could see the gold dome sitting on the big pile of rubble that used to be the Capitol building, and began to work my way toward that. When I was next to the dome, at the top of the hill overlooking what used to be the outer edge of downtown, I gazed down and saw some tents set up in Civic Center Park, across from the Capitol. I was so relieved that others had the same idea of coming here and that there might be some organization already in place, that I almost wanted to sit down and cry. Instead I looked at my immediate goal, an intact portion of the bottom steps of the Capitol, and spied the most beautiful person I have ever laid eyes on, sitting on the third step up. A large wolfhound sat motionless on either side of her as she brushed her hair. She had long hair that seemed to shimmer with multiple colors of blond as she brought the brush through it. I am sure she had to brush it despite the rain because it was so thick.

As I slowly came forward, she stood. She was tall, close to six feet. Her facial bone structure was like a sculpture. She smiled at me encouragingly, enlivening her features. As I got closer and our eyes met, I saw hers were a dark violet. I felt a reaching out of her mind toward mine as we made eye contact, and I let my own mind reach back. There was a solid energy connection between the two of us that felt like it hooked into place.

The dogs didn't move as I approached. They were gazing at her, and then glancing at me, as if waiting for her command. I am embarrassed to say I found her so stunning I could not take my eyes off of her, even as I picked my way toward her. I have always been considered very attractive by others and have had some beautiful friends, but she was truly perfect, more beautiful than any movie star I can think of.

I finally reached her and we were face to face. I quickly glanced down at her pack, and resting on top were an AK-47 and a huge serrated knife, very shiny. It scared me and I quickly looked back up at her face. She beamed a smile at me that contained such goodness and kindness I almost wanted to cry again. Then she said, "Nice backpack," and we were instant friends. Between the odd energy connection, the dogs, the gun and the knife, her surreal beauty and the hair brushing, it was so like a scene out of a movie I almost wanted to turn around to look for her action-hero counterpart to come striding onto the scene.

Her name is Isolde, and it turns out she does have kind of an action-hero counterpart. She is waiting for her twin brother Ian. Her being a twin made me like her all the more.

She gave me a little information about the setup in the park. She told me where her tent was pitched and encouraged me to set mine nearby. What a bonus to meet someone I like and have an odd palpable connection with. I am sure everyone feels that about her because they want her to like them. It is funny to experience this from the other side. I have always been considered attractive and I know I am very smart. All my life, I have been raised to concentrate on what is inside, not outside. Especially intelligence. Because I am an attractive doctor, I think I get a certain amount of attention or deference or something that many people may not. It is hard to explain, or even put my reaction into perspective for myself.

On another note, I was so glad to have brought my light backpacking tent. Again the selfish part of me that is glad I have my own space that is too small to share.

There is almost no organization at the park. A large, timbered canopy that has sheets hanging off three sides to keep the rain out is the central gathering place. The shelter is ringed by camping tents of various sizes, shapes and condition. A small fire glows in the center of the shelter, and there is a post with a sheet of paper nailed to it that you can add your name to indicate you have survived. I guess it has to start somewhere but seems a little ridiculous -- but I did add my name to the list of survivors.

Some brave souls were going out to see if they could find anyone who needed help, but mainly, like a herd, we huddled under the canopy on makeshift chairs and blankets. It was nice to be around other people after the long stretch by myself. The fire was somewhat cheering and added an element of camaraderie. We all talked in low murmurs, as at a funeral. In a sense it was, as

I am sure we have all lost someone.

It seems that people here, like me, have enough food and water for a few days, but I wonder what happens when everything starts to dwindle. Now, everyone is cooperating because there are so few of us and we are glad to have one another. Everyone seems to be waiting for someone or waiting to go somewhere, like myself, but I am betting, now that things are settling down, that we will be seeing more people. I wonder if we are going to see more injured. There are people here that have abrasions and some minor injuries, but nothing life-threatening. I guess if you are badly injured there is no way you could make it very far.

No one so far has come from anywhere but Denver so I don't know what the roads leading out are like. Isolde said her brother is coming from the mountains, so I am anxious to see him. I am sure she is, too. She said if anyone would be able to make it anywhere, it would be Ian. I get the impression her family is wealthy. She talked about Ian coming from their family house in the mountains where she apparently lives. She said she had been staying at the apartment the family owns in Denver (What kind of apartment would accept those two huge dogs – although they are remarkably well behaved) so that she could visit with her parents. They had been traveling from their home in California and had stopped in Colorado on their way to Washington, D.C.

Tomorrow we hope there will be more organization. Toward 4 p.m., word came that there has been contact with the governor. A couple of plainly dressed but clearly military guys were going around the various camps with the information that the governor is safe and well and in contact with other leaders here and throughout the country. There has been extensive destruction throughout the world and communication is limited, they said, but they are talking about how and when the military should be called out. There will be further contact tomorrow evening, they said, and hopefully more contact and information as the days go by. For now, a very limited number of special forces are out and about, surveying the situation and making contact with survivors. They said there are other survivors, and people are beginning to emerge and gather at places such as churches, schools and intact buildings.

This news cheered all of us, and we started talking about what we need to do to start rebuilding the world. Laugh. Gathering medical supplies is at the forefront of my mind, along with food and water. We talked about setting up a latrine location so piles of crap do not suddenly become an issue. Humanity marches on.

For now, I am relaxing in my tent. It is nice to hear the sound of voices nearby and know that there are other nice, normal people who have survived. We have agreed to get together later tonight to come up with more formal plans and talk about other things that will probably have to be addressed. Like digging out the dead before decomposition gets too bad. Or the fact that if the rain keeps falling on these downed trees we are going to have a mushroom problem of epic proportion. I have to stop thinking morbidly, but it is hard not to when I contemplate the mass destruction.

Someone suggested we do a campfire sing-along after we get done setting up housekeeping around here. Everyone is to try to remember all the words to a favorite song. We can all sing and keep ourselves cheered up. The kids will love it, of course. I remember the lyrics to a lot of folk songs, so I am looking forward to that part of the night.

I am going to spend some minutes just lying back with my eyes closed. I want to relax and think of Mark and the kids. I want to spend some time being grateful that all this is going to work out. Things really could have gone south for me at any time within the last few days, but here I am, safe and sound. Then I will have a bite to eat, a walk around the perimeter to see what there is to see before I head over to the canopy for the housekeeping meeting and sing-along.

Day 3 6:38 a.m.

A loud drunk stumbled into camp this morning. He said he has been drinking and wandering around for a couple of days because he has nothing to live for. I guess some things in the world never change. He said he had come from Denver International Airport and was talking as if there might be a large group of survivors out there. I hadn't thought of all the stranded travelers, and it would make sense that DIA, which was so recently built, would hold up to anything weather-related. He said he came down the Interstate 70 corridor, and the highway is badly buckled and broken and there are many, many cars littering the entire stretch. He said other people are out there on the main roadways, and groups are camped on the sides of the road.

It is good to know things are somewhat navigable out there. I am planning on helping out around here a little this morning and then striking out for the cabin. The sing was great last night. We were able to forget our cares for a while and bond together as survivors of this catastrophe, but there isn't much reason for me to stick around. It sounds like things are going to be up and running soon, and although I really wish this rain would subside, I will plan to layer up and go. I am scared to make my way up the road over three mountain passes and into uncertain territory, but this is my plan. I think there are probably people out there who could use medical attention, but I don't necessarily think it has to be my duty to search them out. I will help anyone who needs assistance along the way.

Everyone I have met here at Civic is nice and normal, and I have every reason to believe everyone else I will encounter will be, too. If not, I have my trusty firearm.

I'm babble-writing because I don't quite know what to do.

I guess I will self-assign the task of making my way to a nearby hospital to see what I can gather in the way of medical supplies today to help organize this camp. There was a suggestion that we set up a supply tent of some type, so I will take anything I find to the supply tent and, at the same time, stock myself up in case I encounter anyone out on the road who needs triage.

11:38 a.m.

I am shaking so badly I can barely write.

As we were setting up the supply tent today, a group of people dressed in camouflage and hunting-type clothing came to the camp. I mention the clothing not because it does not make sense for the weather but because their entire group was wearing some form of it. The energy as they approached was brutish and controlling, and was coming off them in waves. They approached quickly across the small encampment but came up short when Isolde and the dogs began walking just as quickly right toward them. A few of our guys fell in behind Isolde, and suddenly there was a feeling of a major faceoff in the middle of camp.

A burly fellow from their group stepped forward and stupidly said, "Who is your leader?" Isolde asked if he were joking or something. Then he demanded that we surrender any weapons and supplies we have. I think we were all in shock. No one responded to this ludicrous suggestion. He took a step forward, the dogs began growling low in their throats, and Isolde pulled a handgun so quickly I couldn't even say from what part of her clothing it came. She leveled it at his heart and said in a voice that held not a trace of a waver, "I will kill you if you take a step farther."

Then the oddest little thing happened. It was as if time stood still for half a second and we all saw the vision of a bullet flying through the air toward his heart. Then the vision was gone and we all blinked a little, it was so fast. I could tell everyone had seen the vision, as it had the effect of making their group physically take a step back, almost as one, and I could feel their group energy dissipate.

Then the big one said something like, "This isn't the end of this matter. We are a powerful engine of the military, and we are going to get everything secured and up and running smoothly. We need to protect what we've got." As he spoke, they were kind of backing away, walking off. I could see them looking at us and our guns, seeming to assess what kind of firepower we had. Isolde said something like, "Don't come back and make me use this. Hasn't there been enough death and destruction for you already? The governor will have a plan."

And it all felt horrible, horrible.

We quickly formed the camp into a tighter setup that can be more easily guarded. I cannot believe this is happening already. I knew there would be an agenda or maybe even competing agendas, but this is too strange and complicated. What kind of military "engine" besides regular military is out there wanting to take over? What is left to want to control? I don't need to be protected, do I? Did some other superpower survive unscathed, and they plan on trying to take over the U.S.? A group who is demanding our weapons and supplies cannot have my personal best intentions in mind. I will be guarding those myself, thank you very much. Unbelievable.

I have got to get a better backpack and get out of here. Or are there bands of roving camo people everywhere, demanding weapons, or conscripting people into service or something? This sucks so badly. Their energy was awful -- so domineering and brutish and dim. Thank goodness for Isolde and those dogs. I don't know where she comes by that bravery. I am embarrassed to report I shrank back as those people approached. I probably would have handed my gun over.

Our plan for now is to leave camp in twos to spread the word that the governor has been in contact and we await further instructions from him and the real military. No one need do anything against their will. We will also try and find out more about these camo people. I don't want to be some kind of freedom fighter. I just want to see my family again, and soon.

7:45 p.m.

It has been an exhausting day. After we got the camp secured, we spread out from Civic Center in pairs to talk with anyone we could find and see if we could find out more about what was happening in other parts of town. The coward in me was happy to be partnered with Isolde and the dogs. We walked toward downtown, which resembles a massive, unstable ghost town. We could really only walk around an outer perimeter of debris. There isn't a tall building left standing, and the barrier looks impenetrable. We met a couple of people wandering around who did not know anything, and we directed them to Civic. It felt productive to be out, but it also brought home how overwhelming this is.

A few of us gathered back at the canopy in early evening and discussed what we had found. Camp swelled while we were out, and it was a little awkward to crowd into the canopy shelter and have people standing outside, straining to hear everything. The neighborhoods east, where I came from, have many survivors, as does DIA. Our mission this evening was to put the word out to beware of anyone demanding weapons or supplies, to clear and create roadways where possible in addition to letting anyone you see know that we have been contacted by the governor and expect further communication today. I think we were also spreading the word that Civic Center would be a central gathering point for information. It was a productive day, and I felt we accomplished our goals and more.

The camouflage group had been around to many of the other makeshift camps. (On a side note, I don't know why I was surprised to learn that the majority of people who survived so far and needed shelter had chosen a church as that place. Churches are known for their large basements and sharing, caring ways.) As it stands now, many people were bullied into turning over their weapons and supplies. Other people did not have any weapons or supplies other than some food or water, and the camo group had the grace not to take that.

This evening, a serious Secret Service type came into camp alone to give us an update. This guy was seriously hardened, much tougher-looking than the plainclothes guys who came before. It made me think he has seen some war zones. He let us know the governor is still at an undisclosed underground location and will not be moving any time soon. As of now, the governor is the highest-ranking official we know of in the area. There has been contact with officials from Washington. Many leaders have survived and also are in undisclosed locations. No organization by the military has been authorized, but the government has heard of this group calling itself military and demanding arms and supplies. We got a report of who they are and what the government believes they represent. They seem to be rogue militant survivalist types who had been loosely linked via web sites and underground conferences and survival camps that talked about how to band together as a militia in times of trouble. Their main organizational tool was an e- newsletter that came out weekly and had a subscriber base of at least two million and maybe much greater. They are more legitimate than other fringe groups in that their subscribers tended to be better educated, their events better organized and their loyalty to the core group very strong. Fringe militia-type groups probably would tag onto a group like this through Internet bulletin boards or chat rooms. From what we understand, as the catastrophe loomed, the newsletter was growing more directive of what the members should do, and first and foremost was to gather weapons and supplies from the general citizenry. They actually had two different long, instructive interviews with a high-ranking general in a couple of their last newsletters, but it is unclear how they reached him and if the general was merely answering basic questions about survival and the aftermath or if he is affiliated with or even leading this group.

I don't like that they might be organized or have

legitimacy, or that they might be affiliated with a high-ranking military officer. I think people will be able to organize on their own, without military overseership of any kind. I don't want to be led or to give up control of my future. I want a say in how this aftermath is going to be set up.

For now, authorized military forces are doing flyovers of the country to get an overview of the situation, and they have special forces on the ground gathering as much information as they can. No one in the government is making any sudden moves, and the manpower does not exist to go after this camo group.

After the report by the military guy, we voted on the best way to proceed here in the park. We set up a guard rotation, and then we all talked a little about how we would like to have things organized in our camp and in the future in general. Someone threw it out there that it seems a little odd that so many high-ranking officials seem to have survived and that they have already been in communication but have not been seen. That kind of resonated with me. I guess the government would have to have safe locations for its elected members for just this circumstance and they would have to stay there until any sort of threat had passed. I, myself, have a reinforced room, so it is not like I did not sense something was coming. Right at the edge of my consciousness, though, something registered. Did they have a better idea of what was coming than regular folks did? Is there some sort of grand plan in place here? I hate having to think like this. A couple of other people mentioned that it was hard to tell what direction those military guys were coming from. And where did they and the highest leadership in the land weather the storm? And who is really issuing commands?

Then, thankfully before we could get all worked up, Isolde spoke up and suggested she lead us all in a meditation for peace. We all welcomed the suggestion, because I don't think any one of us wants to rile ourselves up about all this right now.

The meditation was very non-denominational. It started with a focus on breathing, being in the present and focusing on breath coming in and out. Isolde gave instruction about how, when your mind wanted to wander, to bring it back to the intake and outtake of breath. Then she gave instruction to add four words to the intake and outtake: "Yod Hey Vah Hey." She said you could say the words in your mind or out loud under your breath. The idea was to use the words and the repetition of the words to focus meditation and let the words bring you to your center when needed. She did calming exercises and some generalized positive visualization about healing and peace and solidarity. At the end, there was a five-minute period of quiet time to either pray or reflect or simply draw in calmness and peace. It was very centering, and the energy was very peaceful. I am such a sap, and it affected me so deeply I was crying at the end. It was a release, and I wasn't the only one crying.

Then we all parted to go our own ways. No happy sing-along tonight, even though it was such a fun bonding experience and might have served to lighten the mood. Everyone has been on edge and needs to get their rest.

Tomorrow morning, I am partnered with a guy named Jon on the 4 a.m. perimeter patrol. He was here before I got here and was one of the first guys going out to see if anyone outside Civic Center needed help. He was also one of the guys who fell in behind Isolde during the faceoff with the makeshift militia, so I am confident he will have enough bravery for both of us if needed.

Our camp has been attracting all sorts of critters in addition to people. I have, by default, acquired a limping German shepherd we named Kevin, who wandered in. Because I am camped next to Isolde, the dog mostly tries to hang out with the wolfhounds but will look for something to do when he is not sucking up and always is glad to take a short walk or get some head rubs or lie at my feet. I feel grateful to have his companionship. I am glad to see the cats are coming back out, because I have personally seen a rat near the trash area and have this picture in my head of the rats being the end-game winners here. The dumb people fight over the mess that is left, leaving nothing but carcasses and open space for the animals.

Wow, that is some tired thinking and writing. I don't even

think that makes sense. Now I really am too exhausted to write or think straight. I am too tired even to cry. I did not think that was possible.

Watch was fairly uneventful. It involved patrolling the perimeter of the tents and then patrolling the outer perimeter of the park. Jon and I would go separate ways, walk the circles and meet back in the middle, then start all over again. That lasted for three hours.   There were a lot of people up and about because, whether on patrol or not, we are all on high alert.

I welcomed a new group to camp and had one of those instant-connection things happen with the leader of that group, whose name is Reginald. It is funny; as people approach, you can actually feel the energy they project. In many of these people I see myself as I was just two days ago: Stunned, looking for a safe haven. Reginald was coming toward me, leading a large, multi-generational group of Hispanic people. Because he is very tall, our eyes kept meeting as the group made its way toward me and it was almost the same instant and solid connection as when I met Isolde. It is hard to describe. It is like the eyes meet and the connection happens and then deepens and it is like you know that person well, you just haven't seen them in a while. I don't know how to put it into words. He seems really quiet and did not talk much to me despite the connection.

I did not realize quite how tall he is until he got a little closer but he is about six-foot-seven, and even though he is wearing as many clothes as the rest of us you can tell by the way he carries himself that he is solid muscle. His demeanor is reserved but very commanding, like he is comfortable with leadership or like he is used to being followed. But the leadership energy was the loving, caring variety, as if he were shepherding his own family. The group was clearly a family or families, but I don't know if he is related to them or how he knows them. He does not look Hispanic, but he spoke fluent Spanish.   We spoke briefly and I gave him the basic camp information, and then he turned around and slowly relayed everything in Spanish to the group. He turned back around, gave me a nod, and began to walk toward the canopy, which we now use as a relay station. As they passed, the people in the group were saying "thank you" and "gracias" and nodding at me, and I was smiling back at them and saying "welcome." I could see the relief in their faces and I was remembering my own recent journey and was so glad they had arrived safely. It was an emotional moment, and many of us had tears in our eyes.

We set up a housekeeping agenda last night and had decided to turn the canopy shelter into the central information station and processing and relay station. We put a process in place for when people show up to camp. We get them medical attention or whatever type supplies they need right away, and then get them situated in a camp spot and show them the central gathering spot, which is now the amphitheater, and the trash and latrine facilities. After we set up housekeeping, we came up with a list of tasks we felt needed to be done immediately and then volunteered for those tasks.

Today, we are upping the activity level. We are continuing to gather supplies and spread the word about hearing from the government, and also letting people know to start thinking of how they want things to be run in their general area or wherever they feel they might settle for a while. There is still no sign of organized military or elected leaders, so we are going about this on our own, at least here at Civic. We will split into teams again, and different teams will look for different items or perform tasks, helping anyone in distress as we go, of course. Isolde and I are teaming up again, with our objectives being medical supplies and canned goods. We have to locate wagons or fashion some sort of conveyance.

These are always times I think of Mark. He could so easily put this type thing together and it would end up being ingenious because he is brilliant. I have so many things stored up I want to tell him, and sometimes I pause and think of what he would do in a given situation. I guess I used to do that anyway. Then I try to picture what he and the twins might be doing, and I feel as if I can almost get an image of what they may be doing at any given time.

5:55 p.m.

It was a great day because there was no sign of the camouflage group. The big news of the day is Ian's arrival.

On the way back to camp for what was to be our last run of the day, Isolde and I saw the wolfhounds actually perk up and look really excited. They are amazing dogs. They are so mild-mannered and well-trained that it has gotten so I almost don't notice them. They are Isolde's constant companions. They are so completely attuned to her they don't seem like regular dogs. They don't react to anything. They don't make an effort to be friendly and doglike. So for them to begin to go on alert and sniff the air and act excited was odd. Isolde then got really excited and practically skipped back to camp. She could not settle down when we got back, knowing Ian must be close but not knowing what direction he might be coming from. We could not figure out how he could be so close that the dogs sensed him, but he was not there yet.

The dogs finally caught a scent and went running, with Isolde close behind. Ian was limping and moving slowly, which explained why it took him so long to arrive. It was quite a picture Ian and Isolde presented as they walked toward camp, both tall and majestic and beautiful and surrounded by large frolicking dogs. Ian looks like what I imagine the god Apollo would look like. Actually, a painting of a Greek hunting scene came to my mind at one point as they were making their way toward me. His charisma is palpable, and even though he was visibly in pain he beamed a smile as he slowly made his way into camp.

Ian's leg was splinted and tied in a couple of places, but he did not want any of us doctors at camp to take a look at it. Isolde had his backpack on her back, and I seriously don't know how he could have borne the weight with that gimpy leg.

There was an indescribable depth of love between the two of them. It was amazing for me to see adult twins interacting. The only twins I have really ever known are my own. It was wonderful to see Isolde so happy. She said she knew Ian was alive, that she could always feel his energy; she just did not know when she was going to see him again.

Ian also has a dog of sorts. Ian's dog is a wolf dog named Rue. Rue looks way more wolf than dog. He is immense and has yellow eyes that look right through you. The wolfhounds were clearly beside themselves at seeing him. The other dogs in camp were actually whining in fear. Some, including Kevin, finally crawled toward him on their bellies in some sort of submissive maneuver I had never seen. Isolde and Ian let everyone know not to approach Rue. He is not like a real dog. You can actually feel his energy and intelligence. Rue paced around the camp; got his bearings in about two minutes and then loped off toward the downtown area.

As a group, we could not help but cluster around Ian, as he is the first person who has come from a far distance. We all wanted to know what his journey had been like, and the kids were not going to let him rest until he told the story of how he came to have a wolf, so he briefly told us the story of his trek down from the mountains and then the story of Rue.

Ian said he would not have made it down without Rue. Rue instinctively seemed to know which route to take or when the ground was unstable or dangerous. At one point Rue physically blocked Ian from walking off the edge of a precipice that was neatly obscured by a normal-looking strand of aspen. They saw all sorts of wild animals out of their element and acting strangely, but thankfully the wildlife gave Rue a wide berth.

Ian said there is major physical destruction of the roads in the mountains. It is as if they never existed, he said. The mountains are steep and debris has nowhere to go but down, so boulders and trees and mud and rivers of descending water have

29

flooded everything and the landscape was at its wildest. Ian and Rue followed what was left of a road when they could. Mostly they picked their way down next to running water. He found a couple of towns on the way down, with not much stirring. Then, as he got lower in elevation and closer to Denver, he started seeing more people and more mobilization.

I was surprised he kept at it, especially after he hurt his leg. After hearing the report, I have to admit to myself that it doesn't sound like someone like me will make it up and over three mountain passes. Not just yet anyway. I am disappointed and yet relieved in a way.

The kids in camp were fascinated with Rue and wanted to know how Ian had a wolf as a pet and a traveling companion. Ian told them that Rue was definitely not in the category of pet. Then, he told the story.

Rue was found about three years ago by the wolfhounds while out on a hike near their home in the mountains. Wolfhounds used to be bred to hunt wolves, and the wolfhounds picked up Rue's scent. Rue had been seriously injured by something but the dogs did not answer instinct and move in for the kill because he is so big. Even wounded, lying half buried under a rue bush, he was menacing. It was a sign of his intelligence that he had rolled in the bush to collect its scent on his coat and then laid down under it. Rue has a strong scent, which would repel most animals. He let himself be nursed back to health in the wild and consented to follow to their house in the mountains. But he would not be coaxed inside.

He is not tame, Ian said. He is not like a dog who will hang around the house to be fed or come if called, but there is a special whistle that he will occasionally come to. Ian said he may have come from a wolf-rescue facility. There are several of those in the mountains. People are always trying to breed wolves and dogs together, and the product is usually more than they can handle. Or, Ian said, he might have been a loner from an actual pack, traveling from an isolated area, looking for a territory of his own, and tangled with a bear or something.

Ian fielded many questions, but it was clear he was beyond weary and perhaps in need of medical attention. He was leaning heavily on Isolde as they left, and I worried for him. He was walking on his own when he came in. He says he has some medical supplies in his pack and just needs a good night's sleep. It looks like he has anything he would ever need in that pack, but I don't know that a good night's sleep will heal what looks to me like a broken leg.

There were all sorts of crazy stories today, many bittersweet. Jon found a little baby, about seven months old, weak but healthy. He survived in a car in his car seat, but the people in the front did not. Sadly, many children have survived without their parents. Kids are small and resilient, and parents tend to protect them best, then go and leave themselves at risk. So we have a few young kids who have been rescued who are now orphans.

One of the saddest cases was actually an older kid. I call him a kid. He is a college freshman who made it home to be with his family. His name is Philip and he was at his grandparents' house with many of his extended family when the entire house was destroyed and he was the only survivor. In one fell swoop, he lost parents, siblings, one set of grandparents and some aunts, uncles and cousins. His grief is so deep and raw that it hangs on him like a garment. Yet he is right there, already volunteering for projects and jumping in to help wherever he is needed. I admire him because I think if I were in his same spot I would be curled in a fetal position somewhere, bawling for the rest of eternity.

For all its inevitable sadnesses, today felt like a new beginning of a sort. We have the new central gathering spot, large enough to accommodate many people, and at any time of the day you can find people there, talking and relaxing between tasks. Camp is fairly well organized now that housekeeping is in place. Today, a team dug out some huge canvas tents from a banquet supply store basement. The tents accommodate what feels like hundreds of people, so we have a new main canopy and a supply tent and a canteen and a medical tent. This place is turning into a well-oiled operation.

We have several doctors in residence, and we will be staffing the medical tent in rotations soon. I obviously have identified myself as a doctor and will be part of the staffing. We are setting up a communications center as soon as possible, and I am hoping to somehow be able to get word to Mark that I am alive and fine. There are search-and-rescue operations running. We are finding people either unhurt or dead at this point. It was that kind of calamity and aftermath.

We are meeting again tonight with the governor's representative for an update. More housekeeping organization is on the agenda because camp is growing so quickly. A schedule of events has been organized and posted. I am happy to report that we are going to do another sing-along at the end of the evening.

For now, I am in my tent, writing. I wish I had enough energy and time to write down some of the other experiences and stories, but I want to spend some time gathering my center with all that has happened and also want to experiment a little on my own with this new meditating thing. I had never really liked meditating or felt like I could do it, but Isolde's guided meditation the other night really affected me deeply and it felt right somehow, so I want to continue to practice on my own in addition to participating in the group meditation. I have been trying to quiet my mind and concentrate on my breathing for fifteen-second intervals when I feel really stressed, and I have also been chanting "Yod Hey Vah Hey" to myself a lot. I find saying those words over and over to myself calming and soothing. For those moments I am meditating, I try to be fully in the present instead of thinking of everything going on and everything I need to do. I think it has helped me maintain my focus and calm in this trying time. Since I feel like I am getting the hang of it and I like it, I will up the time I am trying the focus from fifteen seconds to one full minute.

I am also going to take a moment or two and do what I have termed my grateful exercise. I have found it is important to remember to be grateful instead of mad that I am facing all of this, so I go through a list in my head of all the things I am grateful for -- past, present and future. I like to think of any time that I was grateful about something or grateful to someone, list it and then give quick thanks for everything I have and, of course, the fact that I survived and am healthy. With this grateful exercise, I have gone as far back as my sixth birthday and given thanks for that chocolate carousel cake I had. That cake dazzled me and made me the talk of the neighbor kids that day. Then I spend time thinking of Mark and the babies because they are what I am most grateful for. I love to close my eyes and remember our times together. I tell myself I can feel when he is thinking of me, too. I know our connection is strong and he would know I survived.

I have to make a personal housekeeping list. There are things I need to think of restocking from the supply tent. Toilet paper is an essential that went fast. Toothpaste, because I brought only one trial-size tube. I would love to have one or two pairs of good socks, but those are a premium.

I try not to dwell on what tomorrow will bring. For now, I am looking forward to the report by the government. I want to get to Mark, but I also feel that if there is going to be a need of a defense of values or something, I need to stand for what I believe in.

11:38 p.m.

Twists and turns to this situation.

The hardened government representative came by tonight to give the update report. There is indeed a loose sort of military and militia banded together, and they are being led by a high-ranking general who was working closely with both the regular military and this militia group right up to the end. They are more organized than was previously thought. They have plenty of weapons and supplies since they were well-armed to begin with, and then spent a few days rounding up more weapons and supplies. What is most frightening is that the general who is involved with this group is high-ranking enough and was actively involved enough in the planning for this catastrophe that he literally knows where everything is buried.

When it became clear that something big was physically going down on Earth, the U.S. government began coordinating with the military to put procedures in place to secure elected leadership and the governmental process. This general stepped up during that time and voiced the opinion that he felt he had a better idea of how things should go and hinted that control should be handed over to the military. As activity to prepare for the safety of the government and its leaders escalated, so did his exhortations to do things his way. Nothing had been resolved with him, and he had not been dismissed although he made his dissent clear. He may have turned to this militia group in frustration and worked with their organization to further his agenda, whatever that is – military dictatorship or military leadership? There also seem to be many loyal military men and women in his group who have served in the regular military and then joined his militia and will continue to follow him because they think he has the right plan. We cannot discount the fact that he has been in the military for a long time and probably will have support from many sectors.

I guess, in the aftermath of this huge a disaster, it could really be considered anyone's game. The funny thing is, I don't want to be led by anyone. Not by the governmental leaders who will be coming out when everything is nice and safe. Not by the military being ordered around from underground. Not by a rogue militia-type military led by a former general.

I am beginning to be angry that upper-level branches of the government seem to view us as dumb animals that can be left out in the weather and then rounded back up again to be managed at their convenience. Then again, I might be considered just as elitist with my reinforced room and safe cabin in the mountains. I understand why things have to happen the way they happen. There has to be organization from chaos, and we have to have a system that goes into place sooner rather than later. But I feel our governmental system is so flawed and broken that I do not want to go back to representative government.

Representatives had grown so out of touch and I think most of them were in it for the very generous pay, retirement benefits which included unlimited health care for the rest of their and their families' lives, and unbelievable perks -- rather than to try to help. Nor were they really required to legislate once they got elected to office. Representatives were not required to read the bills they were voting on. I can't even get started about how convoluted the process of legislation had become with lobbyists allowed to influence leaders and legislation that no longer was straightforward. In Washington, there were twenty-two lobbyists for every member of Congress. Lobbyists donated money, threw fundraisers and basically were trying to manipulate legislation. Many of these lobbyists were previous members of Congress and had quite a bit of influence. Nothing was really getting accomplished up on the Hill. The representatives had such a rich lifestyle that they were out of touch with regular people so they probably didn't even know the issues their constituents might have. The system was so old it just wasn't working anymore. It simply was being manipulated by those in power for their own gain.

The entire electoral process had grown so complicated that no regular person could just sign up and run for office and try to change things. In the days of rapid communication, why wasn't there better communication with elected members of government? Representatives had the franking privilege. They could send as much free mail as their office desired to generate. I never received communication from my representatives unless they were using the privilege to solicit for another term in office. They never used those letters to keep me posted on issues that might be affecting me or my district. They could have sent a piece of mail to every household in the country far in advance of disaster, warning every single one of us about what might really be coming. I guess that action would have generated its own complications, but I felt our system was rotting from the inside, like Rome right before the fall.

Now I want to have a direct say about what is going on and how we are going to proceed from here. I know I am not the only one. Reginald had some pretty pointed questions for the government representative that highlighted some of the same things I had been considering. He wondered why there was not better organization for all the people, not just the leaders. He asked why no leaders have shown themselves, or helped dig anyone out, or done a shift boiling drinking water for the people in camp. So far, they are not showing any solidarity with us whatsoever. Is everything going to be left to the special-ops people, the military and the regular people to get everything up and running again, and then the leaders are going to waltz out, regroup and begin issuing directives? Or is our other option this military guy who will set everything up like the military and we will have to take directives from the brutes?

I value the military highly. I love organization and protection and standing together against opposing forces. But I don't want to take orders, especially from the type that came into camp. I want to do whatever I want to do when and where I want to do it. I am responsible enough and smart enough.

We said our piece to the government guy, but he just looked and listened. His face did not change while giving the update tonight, and I certainly couldn't read emotional reactions to what we said to him. He put a one-minute speaking limit on the time anyone was allowed to speak, and then pretty quickly he said we would have to table the rest of the discussion. He said it would be best to organize our thoughts and come up with something on paper that he could present.

He wanted to move on to the findings from the flyovers.

He let us know that the flyovers are indicating huge physical changes to the continent. The United States is now much smaller and actually split in two. The continent split down the Mississippi River basin, beginning at the Great Lakes. The split is two hundred miles across, and the river is raging down the middle. It appears that the Great Lakes might be draining down the basin, so not only is the water volatile but the air currents are unpredictable. The continent has a lot more water than it used to. Huge inland lakes have formed. Both coasts lost big parcels of land to the sea. The Gulf of Mexico has expanded inland. It appears that there has been great loss of life in all areas.

Many of the highest-level elected officials as well as the general and his militia are on the East Coast. The general has strength on the East Coast, since he was based in Washington. There were predetermined safe geographical locations, and it makes sense that the general is going to know where the highest-ranking leadership might be. The general has access to all high-ranking military information. We don't know what he is going to do with it or what he wants. There has been field radio communication between all leaders, and we know the general has the same radio equipment the leaders have and is probably monitoring for information. He has full access to planes, weapons and supplies. So we are in a holding pattern with the regular military. There is a chance he might try to kidnap a high-level official, or he could be trying for a coup d'état. For now, it is just special ops on the ground and in the air, helping to gather and spread information but nothing that might be construed as offensive military action.

Perhaps the general will be in touch and want to coordinate efforts. Maybe he just wants a stronger say in how the military is deployed for rebuilding since no one listened to him before the reversal. Regular people might even want to fall in with his militia because it is easiest and most organized. Many people may like the security of having the decisions made for them by someone who has experience in unstable environments such as war-torn countries. As a high-ranking military man who has seen a lot of action, he has leadership experience in times of great chaos and knows how to get the job done. I am sure he feels he would be the best to lead in this sort of crisis.

We were told that his group has moved underground and is not communicating. They have amassed a lot of weapons and supplies. They seem to be moving toward mobilization on the East Coast. There have been nonmilitary planes crossing the two-hundred-mile-wide Mississippi River. The thought is that they are going to mass on the East Coast, evaluate their manpower and supplies, and then make a move.

What will be his move and why? Why does there have to be inner strife in the not-united United States? Why can't we all just work together, get this mess cleaned up and get back to living our lives? That would be too easy, I guess. I never think that maybe, since the United States is so vulnerable right now, we are ripe for invasion by any country that was not hit as hard and might see this as the perfect opportunity to foist their agenda on the world. Maybe the general feels we need to organize and protect ourselves against something like that.

We were told that the military or reserve will not be called out in full force until we get this situation handled. The regular military was released on the day the newscasters let us know to take cover. There will be a call put out when decisions have been made for them to regroup. I know that will happen, too, as the military and National Guard we have here in camp said they would answer the call whenever it came. They are amazingly loyal people. Special-ops groups are in place now and are handling remapping, clearing, communication, protection of the leaders and various other immediate tasks.

We were all feeling pretty riled up when Isolde strode to the front and suggested another group meditation with a focus on healing the Earth. It was good timing again, and we all agreed that we should be focusing on the positive.

She had us start with the breathing exercise. Intake and outtake. She taught everyone the words again, "Yod Hey Vah Hey," and told the group to repeat the sequence over and over to themselves either in their minds or out loud, slowly. As her voice flowed through the crowd, we could feel the energy changing. We were feeling calmer, and she led us in some general positive visualization. Then she brought the focus in on the Earth as a planet. She had us visualize Earth as if we were looking on it from the moon. The beautiful picture of Earth hanging there in space, calm and peaceful with the blues and greens and floating mists of clouds. She instructed us to reach out and visualize encircling Earth in our arms, blanketing the planet with our loving energy. As I reached out, I really did feel a connection with a Great Spirit. Well, maybe not an actual connection, but I thought I could feel the organic planet energy. It felt primal and powerful and peaceful and somehow accepting of anything. She instructed us to center and ground our energy to the center of the Earth energy and keep that bond in our heart. We have to acknowledge a synchronic relationship with our planet, she said. It was a wonderful exercise, and I feel it gave me a better understanding of the oneness of all things.

Isolde left us with the caution that we need to learn to better control our emotions. In the past, we have let emotions stampede through our lives like wild horses. Break those emotions, she said. Harness them. Learn to judge less, accept more and practice indifference. Meditate. Forgive one another easily. Now is the time to tap our potential and move humankind forward. The energy is lightened somehow, and we need to keep up the positive thoughts and positive interaction with one another, and really use this energy to create good things.

Onward, to the sing-along, which was raucous good fun. There are so many people now that the song list has grown to epic proportions and there are instruments and dancing. Everyone participates, and it is such a kick. It leaves us feeling uplifted, and that is just what we need.

I must get to sleep. I have the 4 a.m. patrol again with Jon. We have become solid friends in my days here. He is always ready to lend a hand or with a quick smile. He is comforting to be around, although he does not say much. Maybe it is because he is an incredible fix-it guy or that he gives off an inventor-like energy. He is an engineer and seems to be able to come up with a solution for about anything. He likes to be busy helping out, but really seems to enjoy finding the key that unlocks a tricky problem. I somehow picture him with multiple projects going on, but I don't know much of his background or what kind of engineer he was.

None of us talks much anymore about our previous lives or

what may have happened to our friends and families and all the people who probably have lost their lives. It is not a callous thing, I think we have all done so much grieving, and there has been so much loss. Those days I spent under the table, crying my eyes out, I was thinking of all the family and friends and extended family I have who might be in trouble or that I might not see again. All I can hope is that if they did survive, they are doing well and not in any pain or danger. Not knowing is somehow a relief, too. When you don't know what happened, your mind tends to hope for the best. There are so many immediate needs, we don't get the chance to sit around and dwell on anything really.

I must wrap this up and get to sleep.

Day 5   7:56 a.m.

I had a surprise guest on my patrol today. Ian showed up at my tent early this morning with Kevin, to whom I am just a memory since Ian's arrival. I thought Ian needed urgent medical attention, and I quickly snapped to. But he was not even limping. When I asked him about it, he tried to play it off like it was not that bad an injury. I could not help myself and kept pressing him to find out how he could have recovered. I know trauma when I see it. He brushed me off with some joke about being a super-speed healer and said he would teach me the secret initiation later.

Then he quickly diverted my attention by asking if he could walk patrol with Jon and me. I agreed because Ian does not have any reserve to him whatsoever. He is wide open, and his energy is big and powerful and fun. I knew he would liven up patrol. Like a little kid he seems to view life as an exciting adventure and wants everyone to hurry up because he can't wait to get on with it. He is so brave, confident and adventuresome that I feel some impulse to try to pretend I am brave too.

As we walked to meet Jon, Ian made small talk by describing his family. He is the eldest of six. He is older than Isolde by 19 minutes. He and Isolde have four siblings. In all, there are three girls and three boys. He told me he wanted me to know more about their family because his parents and youngest sister happened to be with high-level government officials in one of those undisclosed underground locations on the East Coast. They were scheduled to attend dinner at the White House the day after they flew out of Colorado. They had arrived safely in Washington before everything broke apart, and Ian seems to think they absolutely would have made it to the White House and been welcomed and sheltered there or at any governmental building.

Wow. How well-connected or rich do you have to be to get invited to dinner at the White House -- and then maybe end up in a bunker with high-level members of the government?

Ian told me all this because he and Isolde have decided to put together a group and head to the East Coast to look for their family, and they would like me to be a part of that group. So many questions rushed through my mind. How, where and why? Why would they want to try to get across the destroyed continent to the East Coast, why would they want me, and why would I want to go? Ian explained that he was not the type to sit around and see what is going to happen here in Denver. He wants to make sure his parents and sister are not in any danger. He feels that all decision making is going to be done on the East Coast, and he can't just stay here and hope everything resolves itself as he would want it to. He has to be a part of the resolution. He also wants to see for himself what the country looks like.

Ian said his family members know the general personally. They don't see him as a deranged fanatic, as I do. They know him as a competent, intelligent, professional soldier who also happens to be a master tactical planner. He is a man who thinks he is right and believes he is doing the right thing to protect and serve. I think Ian wants to somehow get to the general and speak with him and feels he can somehow influence this outcome. Or maybe he really is such a man of action that he cannot just sit still.

Ian's thinking is that if he puts together a small group, we can travel quickly and still have the safety in numbers. When we make it to the East Coast, he thinks we can begin to recruit normal people like ourselves to the cause of peace and rebuilding. Let's all just get together and talk and get this figured out before someone takes over and we don't like that someone, and if we can get enough normal people on board with peace, we have an agenda.

Why do they want me, and why would I want to join this somewhat flighty mission? I would be the doctor of the group. And my motivation to go? Ian is a pilot and says he will fly me home to South Park when all this has been resolved, hopefully sooner rather than later. He said the way he figures it, I can stay at Civic Center and continue to get everything set up in Denver and hope they get through to South Park soon, or I can go with them.

They are going to head to a regional airport and get a plane. He will do some flyovers first by himself to make sure it is safe, and then we will head over to the East Coast. There will probably be people that want to get to their loved ones over there, or regular people like us when we get there who want peace and rebuilding and working together and deciding as we go along how we want to handle all things governmental and military as a populace, instead of by direct order.

Ian thinks that with as small a population that seems to be left or has so far shown itself, if the East Coast is similar we will find people, quickly mobilize support for this agenda of peace and cooperation among regular people, and it should be pretty safe as we are doing so. It's the same stuff we are doing here: Going to churches and schools and from home to home, and encouraging people to begin to come up with a plan for how they want to be governed. We have to think that the people on the East Coast and everywhere just want to get back to as much normalcy as possible in the shortest amount of time. There have to be people stepping up over there and organizing and voicing the same concerns we have here about how things are being handled and who this militia group is.

So, we all go over there and help mobilize support to get a vote of the people together on how we all want this to go between the military and the government before either of them tells us straight up how it is going to be or gets into a battle over how it is going to be.

And when all that is over and the conflict has been resolved with the general, Ian will fly me to South Park. If we fly a small-enough plane, he said, he is skilled enough to land in a tight space.

He told me to give it some thought today. They want to

leave early tomorrow morning.

Then off he went with Jon when we met in the middle, to put the proposal to him. The group would be Jon, myself, Isolde, Ian and three others. Ian wants to make it to the regional airport and see what is available as far as usable planes and fuel. A regional airport will be more open. He thinks the military, regular and rogue, would have the big airports in their sights, so we would have a better shot at a plane or planes and fuel at a regional or municipal airport. We have to hope that the camo group has not beaten us to whichever airport we choose. Thankfully not many people know how to fly a plane, and you don't typically find the big jets at smaller airports, so we would have that going for us.

Do I want to do something like this? I don't know that I can say no. Like Ian, I want a say in how things are going to be set up. I can't just cower here at Civic Center and hope for the best. I will have only myself to blame if I did not do anything and then disagreed with the outcome. What if the outcome is military-type domination by people I don't like? I don't want this to escalate to some sort of civil war, either. I know why executive leadership would not want to have to order a single member of the armed services to put his or her life on the line in a fight for power and control, or in protection for one of them.

I don't know if the general's group would use a show of force to push for its agenda, whatever that agenda might be. It is so stupid to think a single precious life would make it through utter destruction only to face being shot down in cold blood. For what? Power and control of the bedraggled few people left on this shrunken continent? Or is the general thinking this might be a good time for the United States to enact global democracy and make it a worldwide system to recover with?

A lot to think about and a big decision to make.

We would literally hit the road early tomorrow morning and make our way on foot or via any working abandoned vehicle we could find. I have a two-hour shift manning the supply tent coming up, so I will make my decision as I go through the day. I am signing up for these things because I want to. Well, and because I feel it is the right thing to do, too. And I need something to fill my time. Not because someone is telling me where I need to be at what time and what I should be doing. I would hate that. But organization is in full swing here at Civic Center. It is a regular town, almost. I don't feel I am as needed here as I might be out on the road.

But what physical risk am I facing? There is danger out in the open, of course. The physical destruction will have to be navigated to get to our destination. There's the danger of flying in the plane, not knowing what we are facing when we get to the East Coast, and the possibility of being shot. I guess I could face that eventuality anywhere.

I wonder what Mark would do, and what he would want me to do. I am positive he would make a stand. He would want to make sure our kids grow up in a country that is totally free, just like we did, not ruled by the kind of thugs who came and demanded our weapons and supplies. I don't want to live in a military dictatorship. I don't want my kids to grow up in a military dictatorship. So, I think he would want me to go with the group and try to make sure peace does happen.

At least I know they are safe from this kind of strife. There are so few people in the immediate vicinity of the cabin, and we know all of them. Our cabin sits on fifty acres and our neighbors all have more than a hundred. I have been going out there since I was a kid. It has been in our family since granddad was a young country doctor and a client gave him what was then a trapper's cabin on acreage in payment and thanks for saving his life. Granddad was an amazing doctor. Mark loved the cabin and property almost as much as I do from the moment he saw it. The people out there are tough and wary. They are all heavily armed and would come to one another's defense or band together very quickly. But we think the camo group concentrated on the larger cities and then ran for the coast.

I will have to continue to turn this over in my mind so I can come to a rational decision.

4:53 p.m.

A huge day of planning for me. I made the decision to go, of course. Still no sign of the camo people, which is very nice. I got a new backpack. Hooray. I never thought I could be this excited about a backpack, but this one is a luxury liner. It seems twice as big as my old one and has an inner frame. It also has a lot of nifty pockets for things, so helpful to keep organized. I got it stocked up and ready to go after my shift at the supply tent.

I hear the most interesting stories there. The stories are getting pretty miraculous at this point. A family of six came in today who had survived in their RV, parked in the corner of a three-story parking garage. The entire garage had completely fallen down around them except for this one corner. They were scared even to open the door of the RV for fear it would loosen something and bring the rest of the garage down.

There also was a reunion of a couple who had been married for more than forty years. She had gone to an appointment and then to check on a friend and gotten stuck at the friend's place. He had struck out on foot to try to make it to the friend's place. He did not make it there, but had survived on the kindness of strangers. Their home was destroyed. They are both so old and frail-looking, but they were just shining with joy when they made it to the supply tent.

Then, there is the ten-foot-long alligator. Thankfully trapped at the bottom of a naturally formed canyon of what used to be a creek and is now a large waterway. He has a large flat rock to lie on and is hemmed in by large rocks. We think he must have escaped from the zoo nearby, and he seems content down in his ravine. Or maybe he is injured. People are feeding him and have named him Boo. It makes one think about what happened to all the other zoo animals, especially the other scary ones.

Tonight, we have our first meal in the new mess hall. It is large enough that we can all sit and have dinner in groups. We had to set up three dining sessions to fit everyone. The people who eat first turn around and feed those who served, and the third group is cleaning, and then we rotate.

A beautiful spirit of cooperation has sprung up here at Civic Center. The energy here feels light, fresh and hopeful. I know I personally still feel very hyper-aware. That feeling has not gone away. Not in a jittery way either. It is like I have some sort of built-in, fine-tuned antenna now or something. If you focus on someone, you can kind of tune in to their energy. And if two people are focused on one another or tuned in together, it feels psychic, as though you don't have to have conversation, you just know what the other person is thinking or means without them having to say much.

An example of this would be when Jon and I were walking back together after patrol this morning. I would consider us friends now, and we fell companionably into step and were discussing Ian's proposal in the broadest of terms, but I felt I could feel all of Jon's thoughts and emotions surrounding the proposal because it involved me. This is a good example because Jon is not an outwardly emotional fellow. He is so excited to be going. He and Ian hit it off immediately, and he is thrilled to have a brother from another mother. That is how closely in step their energy feels. They both are the kind of guys that can fix anything, given enough string and a paper clip. They love a challenge and flying by the seats of their pants.

I could feel that Jon hoped I would be joining them but was trying not to influence my decision either way. So I asked him if what I was feeling was true and he said it was spot on. Then I asked him what kind of engineer he was before this because I had gotten that strong inventor impression from him. He told me he was a solar engineer. He owned his own firm, which had developed cutting-edge technologies. He loved his work and was never happier than when he was in his large workroom, coming up with a new or better way of doing things. Solar offered him an endless frontier to explore. He had been married to his work. His company was incredibly progressive and hip. He had treated every single one of his employees very well, using amazing perks to retain all the best and brightest. Every member of the staff got the perks, down to the office cleaner. The perks included things such as free membership to any health club you wanted, whether that was yoga or aerobics, hard-core weightlifting or a women-only gym. Free breakfast, lunch and snacks, and unbelievably, all the food was natural or organic and healthy. They were an almost one hundred percent green office. They recycled or reused almost all output. And the best perk, to my mind: on-site child care and dog daycare. What a great environment to work in. No wonder he retained all the best and brightest. All of my intuitions about him were on target.

We here at Civic Center are all in agreement that there is a heightened sensitivity, it is a good thing and we should put it to good use. We have all been enjoying the meditation exercises so much that the Civic population has set up a large meditation area with a tent and a large open space that will eventually have a garden at the edge of camp to fuel the good energy. At any given hour, you can go and find people there. Already, that area has developed a serene, calm atmosphere you can feel as you approach. I dipped in and out several times today myself.

We gather again tonight after dinner for our Town Hall, as we have started to call it. We vote on the items on the roster, talk about housekeeping issues and then have the sing-along. We put the military guy's idea of the one-minute limit on speaking in place and things run smoothly and don't go too long. And it is no longer just a sing-along. The instrumentation section has really grown, and there are guitars and drums of every shape and size and a brass section. There are gifted musicians and singers here, and the music and singing always is uplifting and fun. After the sing, our group of seven will get together for some last-minute coordination and planning.

I miss Mark and the babies. I am constantly storing up my stories from the day, and picturing what he would say, wondering what he and the kids are doing at this moment or that moment, or what his daily experiences have been like. I know I am right where I need to be, but I surely do miss them and our life together. I miss so many things. But it is not good to think of that.

During a break on the first song night, we made the mistake of going down that road. It started with someone laughingly wishing they could get their hands on some fresh sushi. We all laughed and started chiming in with what we wanted. Then it became a bit of a lament, and we decided that we cannot do that anymore. It is all about living in the present with what we've got.

On that note, I am going to head over to the meditation tent and then to dinner and the Town Hall.

10:32 p.m.

What an interesting group of seven we are. The symbology of the number has not escaped me either. It is to be myself, Jon, Isolde, Ian, young Philip, Reginald and Beatrice.

Beatrice goes by Bea or Tree or Betty or just about anything you want to call her, she will laughingly tell you. She strikes me as the most unstable of the group -- not that any of us is stable at this point, obviously. She is, or was, a massage therapist, tarot reader and herbalist, and she still is practicing all three. She really does seem to be in tune with this new vibration and is quite psychic. She seems way too happy considering this turn of events, as if this is some stage play and she cannot believe she has been so lucky to land such a big part in it. She is over the top and consistently cheerful. That's probably why she strikes me as unstable. She is very pretty and follows Isolde around unashamedly like a dog. When I tried to half joke about this to Isolde, she told me we could all take a cue from Bea and try to live in the moment and see the good in everything and enjoy living. I think Beatrice has extra-special herbs in that healing pouch. I know I am reacting a bit like a jealous twelve-year-old, but Isolde and I really don't get any time together and I have missed her. Any time I might have tried to chat with her, there was Bea.

I love Jon and Philip, of course. They are both amazing. Either will jump in anywhere they are needed, and no task is too big or too dirty.

Reginald is quiet and keeps very much to himself. If you try to tune in with him, you can almost feel him block you. The only things we know about him come from the three families he saved and brought to camp that day. They all lived in the same apartment building. He was an attorney for a black-rights organization and seemed to work all the time. He had kids who don't live with him who came out and played, but the kids are the only people he ever had over to his place. He seemed to work all the time but made an effort to get to know the families in the building and had handled pro bono cases for some of the people or their relatives. In return, they would fix the old beater of a car they teased him about. The ladies would cook for him and leave food by his door if he was working really late, and he would occasionally show up to their Sunday afternoon picnics and have himself a grand (if reserved) time. I am not being a snob, but the apartment building they lived in was in the worst part of town, so it is clear Reginald is not attached to money and status.

He spends time in the kids' tent, and it is the only time I think he ever lets his guard down. He is so genuine with them. I walked by earlier today, and he had about five kids hanging on him and he was pretending to be an airplane and was swinging them around and they were shrieking with laughter. He tells them outlandish stories and sings songs with them. He also puts in tireless hours wherever else he is needed. He lets everyone pick their assignment first and then he seems content to fill in whatever no one else has chosen. And he has an incredible singing voice. He brought the house down tonight with "Amazing Grace." I was crying at the end, of course.

Ian and Isolde are like rock stars here in camp. Everyone knows them, and they each speak at least six languages fluently so they are constantly in demand. Who speaks six languages fluently? They said they had a gift their parents recognized early. And it seems that they had the money to indulge whatever grabbed their attention, not that they ever directly refer to their wealth.

A picture is forming of them and their family through their anecdotes. One of my favorites is how their parents met. Their mom and their dad were respectively the most beautiful people to be born in each of their small towns in three generations. The two were both lauded and applauded by their entire towns all their young lives until the day each left for the bright lights of Hollywood to use their looks and talent to make it big. They met at a forgettable Hollywood party when their dad-to-be stumbled over to their mom-to-be and said, "We would make the most beautiful babies." It was a terrible pick-up line, but their mom liked him anyway and they went on to prove it true. Their dad made it in daytime television and their mom made it in real estate. Real estate and politics do go hand in hand, so I can see how they might have gotten connected politically in California and then maybe the leap to national involvement -- and safe passage to an underground bunker?

Apparently, their grandmother from their mother's side came to live with them before they were born and never left. She sounds like an amazing character: Southern, with pretensions to French royalty, they like to joke.

I don't know if Ian has ever had a job. It sounds as though he has traveled the world from corner to corner, been in some pretty tight situations ad loved every minute of it.

Isolde lives in what sounds like a huge house on the outskirts of the ritziest ski resort here in Colorado. She was the banquet manager for the top restaurant in town. She was not your typical banquet manager at a typical restaurant. This restaurant handled the elite of the world. When the elite want privacy, they hire a banquet room at a ritzy restaurant. The extremely wealthy were booked, as well as celebrities, royalty, high-dollar corporate meetings and especially Japanese businessmen. One of her languages is Japanese and she told us one of her nicknames was "Geisha" because the restaurant began attracting so many Japanese businessmen.

We are a very attractive, extremely fit, highly intelligent group of seven. I think there is something to that besides the obvious, but I am too tired to think it through. We will also be traveling with five dogs: Rue and the wolfhounds and Kevin and a little terrier who we named Benji. I have not seen Rue since that first day. I don't think anyone has but Ian or Isolde. There is something extra comforting about traveling with our little pack of dogs and that huge wolf dog.

We did a brief meditation together as a group of seven, and the energy we generate feels different from the energy our large group of people at Town Hall generates. Isolde said she wanted to fine tune our energy as a group, so she led us through some interesting exercises which built our energy up to what felt like a crescendo in a way. It was more focused and dialed in, and was specific group energy that I had not previously connected to in any of the group meditations.

I think it is going to be harder than I expected to pack up my little home here and say goodbye. I know we are going to try to set a good pace, so I don't know if I will get a chance to write but I am going to try. The pessimist in me wants to write something like, "If I don't make it and this journal makes it back to Mark and the babies – I love you all so much and I am doing this because I want to make sure the world is safe and free. I don't want the wrong crowd to get the upper hand while we are on our knees." Instead of thinking negatively I am going to end on my favorite Irish blessing, and vow to think positively and write positively from here on out.

"May the road rise up to meet you. May the wind be always at your back. May the sun shine warm upon your face (Oh, how I long for that). And the rains fall soft upon your fields (the fields have plenty now). And until we meet again, may God hold you in the palm of His hand."

Day 6 4:32 a.m.

This will be the last time I write holed up here at Civic Center in my little tent. The second secure little world I will crawl out of and leave. I am nervous but excited. It feels good to be doing something that may move this process forward more quickly and get me to South Park. We are leaving with no fanfare. I don't think most people at Civic Center know that we are striking out. Not that it is a secret, but we as a group all kind of kept mum about it. Our plan is make our way on foot until we get to the outskirts of town, where we hopefully can pick up a vehicle, get on the road and make our way toward I-76 and Sterling. Our destination is one of the airports along the way. If the road is badly destroyed, we will go along the main river basin or the train tracks.

I believe we are doing a group meditation this morning that includes reaching out with our minds and "touching" each of the small airports that might be our destination, and also sending the rogue militia group love, forgiveness and healing thoughts. Isolde says in the lightened atmosphere, their old combative energy might just stand out, so we might be able to do an exercise similar to dousing where we look at a map or atlas and let our minds browse over it, and we might be able to pick up on their energy to figure out where they are headquartered -- and then we can go the other way. All this sounds very sci-fi to me, but then again so did magnetic pole reversal.

I-76 makes sense because it gets pretty flat and uninhabited up that way quickly, and there are several airports in the Fort Morgan and Sterling area. Hopefully it's also a highway that was less traveled and will have fewer cars to get around.

12:46 p.m.

We are just outside Commerce City at a truck stop. It was a nice facility at one time, but now it is mostly collapsed. Jon and Ian are looking for a vehicle that will accommodate seven adults, five dogs, our gear and as much fuel as we can possibly carry. It is a tall order, but with that vehicle we are hoping to get onto state Highway 2 from here and then on to I-76. We have heard that Highway 2 is somewhat clear and people have used cars to get to this truck stop from there. We met someone from as far away as Nebraska, heading to Civic Center. The problem with vehicular travel seems to be that when you go off road to get around abandoned cars or buckled pavement, your vehicle gets mired in mud. So Jon and Ian will have to find a vehicle to circumvent that.

It was quite an adventure even to get here. Just outside Civic Center was fairly clear, but then as we got toward the Denver city limits it was hulking debrisville again.

We set off this morning after the group meditation. Those meditations are taking it up a notch. We did the breathing and calming and the "Yod Hey Vah Hey" chant out loud as a group for a couple of minutes and then some biofeedback to keep our physical selves ticking. We did grateful positive affirmations.

Then we sent waves of love to the rogue military, and I swear I could feel their resistance like a wall. Then we reached out with our minds to see if we could get a visual. In our minds, we were supposed to picture a large white movie screen and then let images flick across it. I was getting images of the burly guy who had come into camp demanding weapons. He seemed to be standing in front of a group, ranting. I could kind of scan the group energy, but nothing was very clear. The overall sense that I got from the room was that most of them were not checked in with him. His energy was strong, but it was isolationist. It felt very real, but I wonder if it is a creation of my mind. Isolde said in that highly fraught moment when he was demanding the weapons, I had reached out and kind of melded my energy with his and that is why I can picture him most clearly, and the fact that he has a strong energy. I tuned in to him, and now I can tune in again and I will need to continue to tune in on him. He is my focus, especially for the waves of love, until I can feel forgiveness and love for him. Until no negative emotion gets in when I think of him. No fear, no intimidation, no emotion whatsoever when I think of him, unless it is love and true forgiveness. This is a very interesting exercise for me for many reasons. I have never liked the use of brute force, and for some reason this guy is the ultimate representation of that. Each time I tune in, I feel almost repulsed, but I have to understand that we all go about things in different ways and he has chosen his.

Then we had the quiet minutes where we were supposed to connect with higher guidance and ask that our steps be guided each step of the way. Actions and thoughts echo through several dimensions. This is how Isolde supposedly did her little trick of throwing a thought forward. She said she had used everyone's heightened energy to supercharge an image of that bullet flying forward and project the thought to the group while we were all dialed in on one another. We should all practice the image projection and throwing a thought forward. Our souls seemingly understand this kind of work and know that there are other channels or dimensions besides the physical and that these exercises combined with meditation open those channels wider.

Then we pulled out the Colorado atlas and focused on the I-76 corridor. There are small airfields right outside of Denver but none of them began to feel right until the Fort Morgan-Brush area. There are three municipal airports, a regional county airport and three smaller airports in a one hundred-mile radius of Fort Morgan and Sterling. We have a good shot at getting planes and fuel with seven airports in that small a radius. Numerous landing strips are scattered in a three hundred-mile radius and mostly flat landscape for practice flights. The area is not heavily populated, so we hope the competition for supplies will be limited.

Isolde and Ian saved the most interesting part of the group meditation for the end. Isolde put a red child's ball on the ground between herself and Ian, and they each turned and walked back from the ball about fifteen paces, leaving it resting in the middle on the floor. They then both turned back and focused on the ball. From its resting position, the red ball rose up about seven feet into the air and arced over to Isolde. It hovered in the air for a moment, jerkily rose again and arced over to Ian. The ball would rise and hover, then arc over and hover again. It was smooth if not fluid, but a truly amazing thing to see them playing ball with their minds. Look, Mom, no hands! They said they had always practiced telekinesis and now with this heightened energy, they feel they can get a real handle on it.

Ian told a funny story of when they were about three or four years old and were so excited to show off their new talent they levitated their toy box for their grandmother Mimi, but did not know how to control the energy. In their excitement, when she entered the room, they accidently slammed the toy box into the wall next to the door, missing her by inches and creating a large hole. They got a stern lecture and then remember being kept apart for a few days -- or a few weeks. They learned not to show other people their tricks. They said we should all start practicing telekinesis with something small.

The road was fairly clear as we left Denver. Roadways have been a priority for clearing around the city, so it was fairly quick moving at first. That only lasted about an hour. The constant drizzle is far more annoying when you are out in it all day. We set out walking in twos. I wanted to walk with Ian and find out a little more about how he healed that leg, but he did not pair with anyone. He was moving forward with Rue to see what was ahead. Rue came at his whistle, joined the group almost the moment we departed, looked right through all of us in the way he has, and fell in next to Ian. The wolfhounds and the other dogs were beside themselves to see him, but it is not like they run up to him and jump on him or try to sniff his butt. Reginald and I paired off for the first leg. We are the two quietest of the group, so I think we are drawn to one another so we won't have to make conversation.

We were fanning out and talking with people as we moved along. We talked to anyone who wanted to hear what was going on with the militaries and at Civic Center, which was everyone. We were also trying to find out what is up ahead. We did not see anyone leaving the city; everyone seemed to be moving toward more populated areas such as Denver and its surroundings. Our main goal was to spread the word to anyone that might not have heard that we have been in touch with the government and that there is a good camp set up at Civic Center or DIA. Special ops has been doing the same thing, and most people have seen the flyovers and are wondering when the military is going to get organized, but not everyone has had direct contact.

The landscape is just so broken up. It took us most of the morning to make it to Commerce City, where we are hoping we can find one ride that fits all of us and our gear and plenty of fuel.

There are so many stories already. I wish I had time to write them all, but we might leave at any moment so I want to write about trying out this super-speed healing that I felt Ian might have been referring to.

About two hours into our journey, we came across a drunken guy with an infected tooth. He had not yet run into a dentist, was mad with pain and had been drinking to try to dull it. I had the supplies in my pack to treat the infection and pain, but he was begging me to pull the tooth. It is too dangerous to pull a tooth when it is infected because the infection can spread quickly through the body. The pain medication was not having any effect, and it was so hard to see him in agony. He was also very drunk, so he kept staggering toward me when I was leaning down into my pack or talking with someone else. Reginald was talking to some people but kept glancing worriedly over. He finished his conversation and began walking toward me, coming up behind the drunken guy. As our eyes met, I tried the thought projection with him and sent him a picture of grabbing the drunken guy from behind to hold him steady. I actually felt a mental wince from him, but he nodded and moved forward purposefully. I have mentioned that Reginald is very reserved and would hate to ever think he used his size to intimidate or dominate. I could feel those emotions quickly. After Reginald had a good grip, I did something that was out of character for me. I impulsively laid hands on either side of the drunken guy's face. His cheek was swollen and hot, and he had a fever. I pictured the antibiotics blooming in his bloodstream and then rushing to the troubled area like medics to the scene. I told him to send as much loving energy as he could to the area. Then I sent one big rush of loving, healing energy, all the while calling to his higher energy to join in the process of healing. Reginald somehow felt my mind doing this, linked in when he felt it and also sent loving energy.

And it worked!

I am not going to say the infection went away, but it was as if the battle turned very swiftly. His pain receded immediately. The area did not feel hot. The infection was subsiding at a very rapid rate. Thankfully for him and everyone, he finally passed out.

I am beginning to want to figure this speed-healing thing out. Earlier, when I was walking, I was trying to think of what Ian was talking about when he said he was a super-speed healer. It could only mean one thing. You can somehow rev up the healing process. Our body clearly knows how to heal itself. If you get a scratch or a bruise, it goes away. If you break a leg or even lose a non-vital organ, it takes a little longer, but the body will heal it -- hopefully with intervention, but even without, the body can heal itself of just about anything but sudden and massive trauma. How to speed the process? Hence my experiment with my hands and energy on the drunken guy.

If I am honest with myself, I am probably almost as reserved as Reginald, so I might never have tried that in my old life. I know the entire healing exercise worked because a few things came together and I was able to work with the new lightened energy and speed the healing on the infection. It was these several things that came together in the moment. There is my overall healing energy. I am a doctor and know what I am doing, and I have the tools of the trade. I administered antibiotics and pain medication. I project confidence and competence in a medical situation. I projected this to him and he linked his energy to mine in a trusting way. Then it is as if I know what channel to tune into because I have actually used the healing energy as a doctor, so I dialed into the channel and then projected that energy forward, using his higher guidance to help. (We all have a group that works with us on the Other Side; this is a Bea theory, and I don't know much about it yet, but it felt right to use in the moment.)

The final part was when Reginald brought his energy in. His energy is big and solid like he is. The thing you feel with Reginald when he tunes in and lets you tune in with him fully is probably what I would describe as true faith. It is like you can feel Reginald energy, threaded in a connection to light. I think it is what pure faith must be like, an integral part of someone's energy. I don't know what religion he was or if he went to church, but his relationship with his faith is a working relationship. It is so hard to describe, but we all felt it for the first time when he opened up and sang "Amazing Grace." When he felt the healing I was doing was faith-related, he beamed that faith in and I could feel it bolster what I was doing.

So fascinating, the entire experience. I want to spend more time pondering when I get the chance.

My only other medical patient was a transgender with trench foot. She felt so liberated by making it through the catastrophe that she had decided to embrace her choice. She looked great, but her footwear was more fashion-oriented than functional. I treated her feet and got her a good supply of socks together so she could rotate at the first sign of wetness. Then Philip gave her his boots. Philip did not hesitate to hand over his lovely waterproof boots, and then put on his spare pair, which were not as nice. He did not do it because he felt it was the right thing to do. His energy was pure concern, and he wanted to make sure her feet stayed very dry. I never felt a twinge of regret from him in his energy. Instead, he was pleased as punch that their feet had been the same size and that he could be of such great help. I aspire to one day be as genuine and giving as he is.

It looks as if Ian and Jon have found a single vehicle for us. They found it at a repair shop behind the truck stop. It had some problem they fixed. It is an outsize four-by-four long-bed truck with four doors, a lift and super rugged tires. It will be a squeeze, but we should be able to fit all of us and our gear but Rue. Ian said Rue would never crowd into a vehicle. He should not have trouble following us, though, as we won't be going fast.

From what we have been able to gather, it will be dangerous to go too far off the road because the ground is so saturated the mud grabs a vehicle and mires it. We are looking at a journey of 80 miles. It used to take an hour and twenty minutes.

7:35 p.m.

We made it to Brush Municipal airport -- not without more interesting stories along the way, of course. The scene on the roadway looks like what I would picture Europe looked like after a bombing during a world war. People are moving along the roadway on all forms of conveyance. Not hundreds thronging as Europe would have seen, but small clusters of people, moving along together, usually pulling or pushing something. More people were trying to use small vehicles, which is good because the road is becoming clear of abandoned cars and debris as people move things out of the way. However, I can see that the roadways are going to grow a little more chaotic soon. We saw a family on bicycles. It looked like a lot of work. One couple was leading a horse and mule that were loaded down with household goods including a birdcage with a bird inside.

We did not stop to talk with anyone since we were driving. It was all about getting here. Outside Commerce City the ground took on a furrowed look. I don't know if that was wind or water or earthquakes. We didn't want to get too far off the shoulder of the roadway because the mud is as thick as rumored. There were several people trying to wave us over to pull them and their vehicles out. It felt bad not to be helpful, but we could not waste time or risk our vehicle. At first it was slow going. We were on the shoulder a lot and almost got stuck ourselves many times when we would have to go around a big buckle in the pavement, a downed overpass or abandoned cars.

Good thing we were so packed in, because there were a couple of hair-raising moments. Ian is like a stunt car driver. He probably did a stint training as one somewhere. Six of us were in the cab of the truck and Reginald, being too tall to fit comfortably in the cab with us, was in the bed of the truck with the dogs. The dogs were under a wood platform Jon had installed that covered most of the truck bed so they would not bounce out, and the gear was rigged atop the platform. Reginald had fashioned a cushioned seat against the cab, and they put rope straps over his shoulders that they secured to the truck so he would not bounce around or out. He tucked his legs under the platform with the dogs. Then they had to put a tarp over the back because of the rain or in case the tires kicked up mud. We opened the back window of the cab so that it seemed as if Reginald were sitting with us. He probably would have preferred that we keep it closed so he could have some privacy.

At first I felt a little panicky, packed in the vehicle, careening around. I had never liked driving or riding in a car, let alone four-wheeling. But I figured that I would not have made it this far only to be taken out in a vehicular accident. I used my meditation techniques and my calming breathing, and then grounded and centered myself.

At some point in the journey, we had a relaxed moment where the truck was barely crawling along and there was comfortable group energy to our quiet. Philip suggested a game of telepathic "eye spy." You pick a person and send an image to that person and they try and picture what you are sending. Then you can begin to give one-word clues if they don't get it. It was a lighthearted little game, and had us all laughing a bit. I could feel our group energy deepening and this little group gathering force somehow.

Then we came upon a terrible sight. We were nearing an overpass. The bridge over the highway had cracked in the middle and the two large slabs of pavement had formed a V on the road. At the smallest point of the V, a car was wedged with its hood facing us. The windshield had popped out, and three bloated dead bodies were extruding outward where the windshield should have been. There was a pause where the six of us in the cab sat staring in stunned silence. We have all seen a dead body or three by now, but this was a spectacle. It looked as though they had arrived at their destination, parked and had been so excited to get there they couldn't even wait to get out the doors and instead had popped right on out through the windshield.

The brief silence was broken when Jon popped an image of a clown car into all our heads and I am ashamed to admit we simultaneously dissolved in a fit of laughter. All of us but Reginald, who was sitting facing the other way and hadn't seen anything. The carnage can seem so unreal. It is as if your mind shuts down or tries to normalize or something. There was clearly nothing we could do for the victims, and sadly they were so bloated and gross that they were featureless and clownish in appearance, having burst out of their clothing. It was still completely inappropriate to be laughing, which had us laughing even harder. Once we had calmed down we got out and stood in a circle and said a few words for them and their families. We thanked their souls for giving us a brief respite of laughter, and I hoped they understood. We covered them with a tarp and Bea put a cloth wreath she made on top of it. Then we got back on the road.

I wondered why each of us had been spared instead of the other person. I wondered if there really was a cosmic plan. I can feel a deeper connection to everyone and to the planet now, and I realize there is so much more to life than I had ever even wanted to contemplate. I had never been religious. I thought science held the answers. Life feels so delicate and so precious now. I want to explore the connection, and I am so grateful to be one of those who made it. I am glad to be doing something that feels right. I want to be more connected. Being a doctor, I used to isolate myself, all the while telling myself that since I was in a helping profession that I was touching others and connecting. Instead I let the MD act as a barrier so I would not have to engage on a personal level with strangers. But I think now we all have to be a little more active than that, more willingly connected.

I never made health a mind-body-spirit connection. I understand now that the body is a vibrating mass of energy that is controlled with our thoughts and emotions. Instead of arrogantly thinking I can control anything that happens to a body with medication, as a doctor I think I am supposed to be more of a mediator of this flow of healing energy, helping the person and the person's higher energy help them. I am beginning to gain an understanding of this on an intuitive and physical level.

For the rest of the trip, we were all quiet and lost in our individual thoughts. The fissures grew longer and wider.

I am practicing developing a touchstone light at the center of myself. I picture it like a serene, peaceful spot that I go to and hang out to chant. "Yod Hey Vah Hey" has developed this calming rhythm for me. Chanting and trying to achieve calmness and peace and doing good in the world feels more right to me than anything. I had always felt guilty about prayer somehow, as though praying for me or the people I loved or the things we wanted or needed was selfish because I had so many advantages that it was not fair for me to get another freebie. This meditation and chanting "Yod Hey Vah Hey" feels more right for me. I need to feel more connected to whatever I believe. Isolde says the four words are the most ancient name for the Universal. The one name for one. That it is not really a name at all. It is an attempt to put a vibration or thought form in words. I don't know if I understand all of that, but I am enjoying how it has provided a cadence for me to focus on while meditating. I would love to have more of a partnership with universality, or at least have a stronger faith.

I pondered what I felt about individual energy and group dynamic energy. Our energy is really strong as a group. Something about choosing to link up and focus. We are together on every vibratory level; we are each vibrating with our various arrangements and rates. Just because we cannot perceive the atoms vibrating does not mean they are not. Everything is a vibration, and atoms are the primary form of life in the universe, or just a building block of the same One thing. A planet has its own arrangement of energy; a chair is its own, a person their own. And we are all one, just vibrating a little differently than the fellow humans because of our unique energy pattern of experiences and thoughts and expectations. So all we would have to do would be to work to achieve greater perception of this energy and how it works. To do that, we will have to move beyond the five senses.

The road grew less traveled as we moved farther from the city. By the time we made it a ways up 76, we saw almost no one. We had to abandon the vehicle and go back to traveling on foot when we reached the outskirts of Fort Morgan. There was water across the highway. The atlas showed a reservoir right above the South Platte River, and we surmised the reservoir had given way and joined the river and some smaller tributaries. The water looked too deep to risk. I was thrilled to get out of the vehicle. We got up on the train tracks like hobos, and the tracks led us right to Brush Municipal Airport. We arrived about an hour ago.

There is an interesting contingent of people here. A group of French people had chartered a large plane, tried to make it back to France and ended up here. There are locals whose homes were destroyed. There are random travelers whose planes were diverted here or who ended up here off the road, such as this really rich guy and his family. He has already approached Ian and offered to pay him to fly him to his huge acreage to see if it is still standing. I guess he has offered to every person he thought might be able to fly him. It seems this is really tight quarters for him and his family, and they are not used to it. The exchange of money for any kind of good or service right now seems so ridiculous as to be laughable.

The people here at Brush have been in touch with the military representatives. A jet flew in initially and told them to beware the fringe militia group that might want their things. They were given the update that the continent has split in two and shrunk. The news scared them, and then they never saw any sign of the camo group. They had had one governmental update since then, and it was vague.

Like everyone, they wanted word of what was happening on the road and back in Denver. They welcomed us. The terminal has some damage to the glass in the main areas and one wing was partially destroyed. They have it set up much like our camp. They have sleeping areas and a main eating hall. They could use more group organization. It is like everyone here is trying to do their own thing within a small space instead of working together to make it more comfortable for everyone. Isolde has suggested a small gathering this evening so she can cover a lot of ground with anyone and everyone who might be interested and show the group here the meditation for peace, and she wants to do a larger group meditation tomorrow. There are people at surrounding churches and schools and parks, as per the new usual, so we want time for word to get out that we are here and have information and want to meditate. Then we will gather for the meditation. It feels like the frontier days, when a posse of strangers would ride into town, bearing a new wind. We have talked to people who have come from up the road, and they say at most points the roads end in water if you are not heading for higher ground such as Denver.

The airport here has one runway. There are twenty planes, which is full to bursting for this airport. Ian is itching to go exploring and find a plane but will have to tamp the urge until we get a better feel for what the people here want and feel comfortable with. The Fort Morgan airport is nearby and has three runways and several planes, and stranded travelers as well. The manager of the airport stayed with it and is loosely keeping things organized. There was movement from that airport in the early days, so we are hoping to get information about who flew out of there and if they talked about where they were going. There is a county airport about ten miles down the road, two small airports within a few miles, and Yuma Regional, which is the farthest.

Tomorrow, Ian will go searching through the hangars for a plane that he can begin to use to test the air currents and see what things look like around us and up ahead. He will practice landing from different directions. He wants to fly over some foothills and some bodies of water to see if the airspace is calm or volatile.

Our goal as a group will be to get over to the Fort Morgan airport and talk with people there and in town. We will be working together here, asking people what their thoughts are about how government should be set up and then asking them if anyone wants or needs to go to the East Coast. We will share our plan of helping spread the word for peace and cooperation instead of military intervention.

Tonight at the gathering, we are going to showcase our Town Hall format and go over how we set things up in Denver at Civic Center as our numbers grew. The town hall format is simple: everyone puts concerns or ideas into a hat or a bowl and a volunteer transfers them to a roster of things to be addressed by the general populace. The one-minute speaking limit goes into place if someone wants to speak to an issue on the roster, discussion ensues and then there is a vote by hand unless it is really close, and then we have some reusable felt cloths, red and green, for the vote. The hat or big bowl goes around and the squares are tossed in, then counted. We'll talk about what to plan for when your population grows in terms of food, shelter and latrine facilities. Another military update tomorrow should give us a better idea of what is happening in the country and the rest of the world.

The group of seven will get together after the informational session and meditation tonight for our planning session and a small group meditation. We are going to practice some lighthearted stuff such as throwing a thought forward and levitating small objects by ourselves and together as a group.

I am tired but fully awake and charged. I can feel the reaching out and the excitement of this group to have some new people in their midst. The French are so excited to hear how well Ian and Isolde speak their language. There might be other doctors here I could discuss the speed healing with. I will have to ask around.

It will be a late night, but knowing we have a free day of sorts here tomorrow gives me energy to enjoy the gathering. Maybe they will want to sing some songs.

11:32 p.m.

It was a great night. I'm so tired, my mind feels zippy.

The group here liked the town hall format, and as far as I can tell has adopted it as their own. The meditation was different in a way. They are not as tuned in as we were back at the park. There is dissonance among them as a group, so they will not all check in somehow -- or it is new to them and they don't have the rhythm of it yet. It is interesting to watch the meditation unfold for a group that has never done this together. Isolde at the front of the room, doing what she enjoys, captures everyone's attention. She is so lovely to look at, it soothes the eyes. She radiates goodness, positive attitude, calmness and peace. She reminds everyone to be grateful that we are together and we are OK. She directs everyone to look inside for strength, wisdom and guidance to move forward, all the while focusing on the positive and goodness and inner strength. As she leads the breathing, you can feel the ragged energy smooth out as people relax. It is as if people become more open and accepting. She then did the Earth-healing visualization -- but that is where it stopped for this crowd. They loved the healing-Earth meditation, and I could feel them connecting through that, but when we moved to the grateful positive visualizations their energy scattered instead of remaining joined. At the end of the meditation, she exhorted them to know this is the time to keep emotions in check and forgiveness at the forefront. Then she answered questions about everything she could in six different languages, and you can see everyone adopting her as their own.

They did sing songs. It was fun as usual and, I think, just the bonding they needed at the end of the night. It is a diverse group of people here.

There are several planes in hangars that have not been claimed by their owners. Those are fair game for Ian. There is a cargo plane that landed here right before the catastrophe and was abandoned, which might be good for our purposes as well. The fuel stock looks pretty solid. Ian will fly over all the airports tomorrow to see what is left in the way of planes and people. I know he is eager to do flyovers toward the East Coast.

Our meditation as a group of seven was lovely. After the unevenness of the larger group, it was nice to circle up and link right in. Even Reginald was more open this evening, participatory if not welcoming. I am beginning to think he and I are very similar in our energy. I think I might also put up barriers when I feel someone try to get in too close. We were all really too tired to do much more than breathing and positive visualization and grateful exercises. We decided to save anything else for the next day. I know it is circumstances such as these that create deep bonds quickly, and already this little group of seven feels as close as a family to me. It is amazing how much I like each member of the group, including Bea. She is not really unstable; she is just herself at all times. She is not a plotter and planner; she lives in the moment.

Directly after the small group meditation, we heard a special announcement on the government field radio that there is to be a summit of sorts at DIA the day after tomorrow. The highest leadership on this side of the Mississippi will be there, and we seven discussed as a group that we really need to figure out who is left in the world, what is going on and how we might want to be governed from here so we can maybe have a voice in the summit. We want to have an active say in how things are going to play out instead of being told. So our group of seven revised our plan to go to the East Coast right away. Instead we are diverting to DIA in the cargo plane to attend the summit. Decision making for the people needs to involve the people. No more closed-door meetings or representatives deciding how we are going to proceed without having consulting and maybe voting first. We can cut out a lot of felt squares for a lot of votes if we need to. Ian initially wanted to offer to fly anyone who wants to go to DIA and attend this summit, but then he figured every single person would want to go. So he decided to radio the government to let them know we would be attending the summit and a significant amount of people would like to come to DIA from Brush. He was to ask if the government would make arrangements to either help ferry everyone to DIA or reschedule the summit. It will be interesting to see how that goes.

We talked a little about what we wanted to accomplish the next day. Most of us will be sticking around here or close to the facility tomorrow morning to help a bit with organization and then in the afternoon see if we can move out and begin letting people in the surrounding areas know there is a meditation and the government is putting together a summit at DIA.

Ian will begin flyovers, and we will have a better idea of where we are headed. Ian stressed the importance of trusting our guts and speaking up immediately if we see or feel anything amiss at any time as we go through our day tomorrow. Never get too comfortable. Someone will need to go over to the other municipal airport and talk with the people there to see if they know anything about the plane that left and the person or people flying it.

There is a rumor that Yuma is untouched, so if Ian finds that to be true we might go there to do light scavenging for supplies. This is a tread-lightly area because we can't have the people who survived in Yuma feeling we are just like the camo people, coming in and grabbing their precious supplies. There will have to be some system in place soon. Currently it is all barter and everyone helps everyone else out. There will be dwindling supplies at some point. They aren't going to be mass producing anything for a long time. From my point of view, I hope we don't go back to that. The daily waste in the medical industry alone was staggering.

We will gather again tomorrow in the late afternoon to report our findings to one another.

Still no word from the general, but we think he is monitoring this same radio channel and must know the government is finally stirring.

Day 7 6:42 a.m.

I wanted to write "Day 7, the Antithesis of Creation." But along the lines of thinking and writing positively, I cannot think or write like that anymore or dwell on what has happened in a negative light. I have to know the planet was just following its destiny, shifting and adjusting as it maintains its place in the universe. It was our fault that we humans got comfortable and built skyscrapers and houses on hills and cities next to oceans.

The luxury of being inside and surrounded by other people helped me feel safer and allowed me to sleep in. But I woke up to one of those strange, vivid and very detailed dreams that tend to happen in the hypnopompic state that precedes complete awakening. In the dream, Isolde and I were flying around in this clear glider-like plane that did not have any kind of propeller or engine. The plane was somehow powered by this big flashing green ring she was wearing. She pointed in a direction and said a few words and we zoomed off. She flew us first over these fields where pandas were contentedly picking a crop of gems. They were wearing these modified gloves that helped them grab and pick, and they were carefully putting the gems in woven baskets next to them. They were working slowly and in sync, and singing a complicated song that involved a lot of clicks between words. This seemed to be some project Isolde was working on, and she told me something about it and then zipped us off to a giant natural amphitheater. It was like Red Rocks but more immense and filled with people of every size, age, race and culture. They were gathering for a big group meditation and were so excited to be there and so happy to be getting ready to start. The best part of that glimpse was how relaxed and peaceful everyone was. There was none of the displaced, homeless-feeling energy that hovers around people since the reversal. In the dream, Isolde was telling me about the projects, the pandas and the great gathering at the amphitheater. Then she pointed again and zipped us halfway around the world to another gathering inside a pagoda-like temple. There was a small group of Asian women, and they too were getting ready for their group meditation. I could feel the love among them and understood that these group meditations were synchronized at the same time all across the world, throughout every culture. Isolde zipped us out of there and started telling me all about how she got all of this going, but in one of those odd dream things her lips were moving and I could not hear a thing. It was as if she were on mute. Her hands were moving and she was explaining and flying us around, showing me all these meditating groups. Then, all of a sudden, she was pointing toward Brush and I didn't want to go back yet but I couldn't communicate with her. I got so frustrated in the dream that I shook myself awake.

Thankfully, I got some instant coffee yesterday. Coffee is the one thing I never want to run out of. I am excited to get my water on the boil and savor a hot cuppa and maybe do some more writing. It feels odd not to have to show up anywhere. I have not been at loose ends since that first morning in my tent in the park, which feels like it was about twelve years ago.

7:12 a.m.

I am at loose ends no more. Bea has tracked me down and asked me to come with her to get some infrastructure set up around here. I don't know how she found me, because I pitched my tent in the farthest unoccupied corner of this place, behind a narrow counter. I am a little surprised that she is tasked, or has tasked herself, with infrastructure. Maybe that is why she found me. I am fairly good at seeing the big picture and bringing it down to the smallest details, and I am glad to help with some organization around here. I would love to get a communication center set up here and maybe get a letter off to Mark if I talk to someone who is braving Highway 285 from Denver into the mountains. So off I go to help set up infrastructure. Not what I had in mind, but hopefully I will have some time to write this afternoon.

5:31 p.m.

Another interesting day, which is an understatement, but nothing is surprising or unreal anymore.

We had some big developments and some smaller ones. The big development of the day for me was learning that Denver International Airport is more than just an airport. It is a small, self-sufficient city that was built and prepared for disaster, so it is one of the safe locations for high-level government on this side of the Mississippi. Our governor and a few governors from other states are there, a few representatives of the House, some senators and the Speaker of the House, who is the highest-level representative in the Mid Region. In fact, the entire executive branch, the House, most of the Senate, many members of state and local governments and many world leaders are still around, safe in undisclosed underground locations. The U.S. leaders plan to meet in the open tomorrow at three different summits, the Western Regional, Mid Regional and Eastern Regional. Afterward, there will be official word about how we are moving forward as a nation.

Bea and I ran into the casually dressed military guys when we got back this afternoon and, in conversation, learned a little about how preparation was organized before the catastrophe. Representatives used the trickle-down effect to warn and not scare people that this was coming. They enacted a few measures and sent some money to state and local governments earmarked for disaster readiness. There were some loose guidelines in place for what to do with the money, and the caveat was that it had to be spent to put the programs in place right away. The buck stopped there, literally. That sounded like the federal government's biggest effort in planning for the masses. I am sure there were others, but I must admit that I feel betrayed. I know that I knew something big was going to happen as well, and I prepared for it, and my immediate family is probably safe, but it might have helped to be even better prepared. And not everyone had a safe place to go. Maybe more action on the government's part could have saved many more lives. I guess there is only so much room in the bunkers.

How could I have been so naïve as to think elected leadership or world leaders would just take their chances and that there would not be big, safe locations around the globe that these leaders would have set up and then scurried to at the first sign of trouble?

Some are now putting forth the belief that the general was lobbying to use the military to get the regular people organized and safe right alongside elected leadership, and that is why no one in authority wanted to listen to his plan. Rumor is swirling that the majority of U.S. leaders were using resources and scrambling to secure themselves and the system, and voted against any measure that might inform the masses more quickly. Even so, I do understand the craziness that would ensue if you told people the world was probably going to end.

Another big development: The guy who grabbed the plane in Fort Morgan is a retired, very high-ranking and well-respected Air Force officer who has been friends with the general for a long time since their meeting on a joint committee when they were in Washington. He had been affiliated with the Air Force Academy and was well liked in the community. He is widowed with grown children, two of whom also are in the military. The thought is that those military guys are going to band together for their own solution because they don't want to take orders from here on out from politicians when, as military men who have brought organization to chaos, they would clearly know how to organize a huge operation so much better. So they are going to organize and do things their way. Maybe they did not like how the situation

74

before the reversal was handled, and they will just do it their way this time. The service people I have talked to all seem to be just waiting for the call. The selfish part of me cannot believe they would stand right up and go back to work for the people who betrayed them. They, too, have endured the crisis, and their families are in as much turmoil as anyone's. They all say the same thing, though. It isn't about taking orders from someone; it is more about organization. They want someone competent to step up so we can go about doing the greatest good for the majority as fast as possible. They just see it as, "Let's get this job done. It does not matter who is holding the megaphone and shouting the orders." They all seem to know of the general, and he is known for his tactical planning. They say it would actually be convenient to organize the rebuilding in a military way because the military has trained together, there are organized procedures in place with which they are all familiar, and they have trained for situations of this type -- nothing on this scale, but they don't see themselves turning into some sort of military drones because the operation will be larger.

Clearing debris and beginning to rebuild is going to be a slog that requires a lot of manpower. They are thinking that maybe executive leadership might fall in with the general's ideas, let him lead the rebuilding effort and then let us all decide together how we want to be governed.

Across the board, we all agree that not one life will be lost to a struggle for power between the two groups. Hopefully the general is working with those medieval brutes that constitute most of his militia and giving them some formal training. Except I can't use descriptive adjectives such as "medieval brute" when I think or write about them anymore because it generates the wrong energy in my own mind and out in the world. I cannot dehumanize them because when you see someone as less than human, it enables you to separate and hold yourself above another and perhaps show them less compassion. If you regard someone as less than human, you might not hesitate to think they don't hurt in the same way you do and deprive them of civility.

Every single human has a soul and feelings and goals. Every single human came here for their soul purpose or to do their soul work or mission, or whatever you want to call that which involves soul evolution. I have to work on my forgiveness and the loving energy that I actively project toward the burly one and the entire group in general. I have to think of them as fellow searchers. Isolde says we must actively and constantly look for the good in every single person we meet. I have to apply the same forgiveness to the government leaders and the feelings of betrayal I am feeling, for those same reasons.

Those are the big developments. One of the small developments is that Ian thinks flying larger planes is going to be safe for long distances. There are no massive wind shears or anything that could take a pilot by surprise. Everything must be manual and by sight because the instruments were blown after the reversal, but he was able to fly several small planes and the large cargo plane without a problem. He did not encounter any other planes in the air, but he thinks the military will want to control the airspace soon. He did small local flights today. He did not want to blow a bunch of fuel, but he wanted to test different weights and then fly farther out and eventually over the Mississippi. So far, only fighter jets and, we think, commercial jets have crossed. He is thinking he will have to fly higher and use the big cargo plane to get across the span of the Mississippi.

When he was doing the flyovers today, he found a young woman with two young children. Her story is heart wrenching, and I am finding it hard to get it out of my mind. She was a nanny for a wealthy family who had a large acreage, their own plane and a landing strip on their property. Ian flew over to the property to check out the landing strip this afternoon, and the nanny came running out of the hangar at the end of the strip. The landing strip is in front of what was left of the house and was clear of any debris. From the air, Ian could see the big, beautiful house sitting partially submerged in the river behind it.

The nanny, Sara, and the mom and dad and two children were all together in a room in the back of the house near the kitchen a day after the boom when one of the kids started wanting a special toy the child had left in its room at the front of the house. The child cried and cried for it, so finally Sara went to try to find it. While she was in the front of the house, the creek behind it -- which the family did not realize had become a raging river -- crested, jumped its banks and began coursing through the back of the house where the family was. Sara was meandering around upstairs when she heard yelling, and by the time she raced back across the house and down the back stairs to the kitchen, the parents were chest high in the water, each holding a child above their head and struggling. The water rose and gained volume quickly, lapping at the stairs where she was standing. The parents basically threw the kids to her and screamed at her to turn around and run. She clutched a child under each arm, got back up the stairs and outside and as far as she could run forward and hunkered far from the house under some trees in the rain for what felt like hours before going back to the hangar where they had been huddled for days. The plane and hangar had been stocked with food and water, on which they survived. She said she might have gone insane with fear if she had not had the children to care for. They were too young to realize what happened and were crying for their parents and wanting to go back to the house.

Sara had no idea what to do or where to go from there. She was so scared that the river was going to continue to rise but she did not want to leave the shelter of the hangar. She felt she was going to have to go back into the ruined house to get supplies and then try to get on the road, and was terrified of the thought. Then the finger of fate somehow intervened when Ian landed there. He flew Sara and the children back with him. Then he went to get Philip. Philip, Sara and the two children have been together all day.

There was another story like that today. A family of three showed up here. They and a few truckers and some other cars had been stranded at a rest area. They were riding out the storm there, and one day there was an earthquake and the pavement buckled under two big rigs and rolled them onto two parked cars, killing the people inside the cars. So some of the people at the rest area made it without a scratch, and others were killed. It goes on and on. I don't understand the selectivity. Why are some left standing while others perish? I am beginning to think it must be your time or it is not. I am sure many died very quickly, but what about others out there, like Sara, who need a helping hand?

But I digress.

Another small development for me was Beatrice and I getting our energy smoothed out. I think she sought me out this morning because I was still finding it hard to like her for some reason, probably because she is just so different from me. She and I spent the entire day together, and I enjoyed every minute of it. I learned a lot and have a new respect for Bea.

The people here asked how we got everything up and running so fast and smoothly back at Civic Center, so Bea and I met with a few volunteers from the airport here to give them a quick overview of how we organized camp and dealt with the first few issues that had come up. They are a lot smaller here, but they have not developed the spirit of cooperation that had sprung up at Civic Center. I think our spirit had something to do with Isolde's gentle guidance and the meditations, so the first thing we did was set up their meditation space. Some grumbled about that, since they lack a lot of usable space. We were setting up a small general supply room and explaining how we had allocated supplies when there was dissension about the way everyone wanted the supplies to be handed out. It was that dissonant energy again, of everyone in this group wanting to do it their way and not being able to see another's point of view or settle on the way that worked best for the majority. There seemed to be three fractious groups that had three strong ringleaders. In the middle of the debate, Bea suddenly called an impromptu town hall and led everyone to the central gathering place. I started dreading it because I know how these things generally go if you have fractious groups: everyone airs grievances, nothing gets solved, and it is a huge waste of time. When we got to the main gathering area, however, Bea began to maneuver the room. She chirped her happy, zingy way through the small crowd that had formed, grabbing the rich guy's wife by the hand and leading her over to plop her next to a very quiet family from town. Then she took the ringleader of the French contingent and sat her next to the family that had come from the rest area. She led the ringleader from town toward the front, and I could read his body language saying, "I have won. Here we go. Now they will finally have to listen. She is taking me to the front so I can speak to the crowd to tell them how we are going to do this." She sat him with the children on the floor in front, and then had everyone sit. She leaned in and grabbed the hand of an 11-year-old French boy and led him to the front of the room. The child was embarrassed to be brought to the front, but she was just talking about nothing and everything as she always does and arranging two chairs facing one another. As I have written, she is very pretty and very psychic. I felt she had correctly picked the ringleaders and diffused the dissonant energy by separating them from their groups. The French boy is so polite and his English is excellent, so Bea drew him out with questions about what he had been learning at school and then asked him some leading questions about why he thought people did not get along. He still had that kid perspective, and his responses rang clear and true. The questions she was asking indirectly pointed out what was happening between these dissonant groups in such a funny way because kids have a way of cutting to the chase. Once everyone was laughing and there had been a few "ah yes, that is true" moments from people in the crowd, Bea began asking the boy for his ideas on ways to get along and get tasks accomplished. Once again, his childish answers were right on the mark.

The ringleaders, cut off from the power source of their group, could not bring the dissonant energy in, and there seemed to be a moment when there was a group realization that if you were going to be here for a while, things were going to have to work. It can be a smooth, relatively painless process or it can be a rocky, uncomfortable road. Their group energy was starting to come together.

Bea then did something startling to me. She told everyone

in the room to turn to the person next to them and tell them one highly personal thing about themselves, keeping it appropriate. Bea went first, faced the boy and said, "I lost my mother recently, just before the reversal, and I want my positive attitude in life to be a testament to her raising of me and the way she taught me to live my life." Instead of asking the boy something personal which would have embarrassed him no end, she turned to him and said, "Now, go hug your mama."

She explained that now it was everyone else's turn, and then beamed the attention on me by asking that I time the exercise on my watch. It needed to last no more than a minute. She said all of this in a very matter-of-fact way and then bounced over to the group of children and sat with them to lead their discussion and work with the town ringleader. Bringing me in when she did was smart. It served to divert the attention, and I seem to have that authority-figure energy, so she knew everyone would feel compelled to follow through with the request. It also kept me from having to do the exercise which she had to have realized I would have never participated in. I started my watch, and everyone obligingly shuffled about to face one another and reveal something personal. It brought a quick closeness to the room that had not been there before by humanizing everyone. The group energy really linked in then.

Bea then cautioned them to keep everything in the open by posting all issues on a bulletin board instead of talking behind their hands. Say only positive things one hundred percent of the time, she said, or do not say anything at all. Begin each town hall with meditation and a true desire to work things through quickly and smoothly. Gain the commitment of each and every person to be on board with the goals, because they want to move the process forward and have it be a pleasant and rewarding experience.

Bea really is an open book, and being with her was fun. Because she has a fun personality, she made every experience we had today an enjoyable one. When my mind would reach out to hers, it felt like there was a welcoming hostess at the door, glad to show me around her nice place. She, like Isolde, has been psychic for a long time, since she was a child. She said she remembers being surprised it wasn't the norm. She said her literature-professor mom taught her early in life to choose your attitude and that life should be treated as if you are on a delightful vacation that you saved up a bunch of money for and have anticipated for a long time. The most important goal is to captain your own ship at all times, keep that ship right and tight, and don't worry about how others are sailing their boats. Don't spend a single moment worrying about what others are thinking, or thinking of you, because it is a waste of time. You can never really know. Instead, do the best you can do every day, every moment, so at the end of the day when you reflect, you are pure of heart. Bea says she has known for a long time that a great shift was coming. She did not realize it would be as literal as a physical shift. She is thrilled with the new lightened energy, and reminded me gently to be more open. When she said that, I actually felt my mind close up like a bear trap. She actually felt it too and laughed out loud.

As we walked back after the impromptu town hall, she talked about reincarnation and threaded in the fact that she knew she was monopolizing Isolde but that it had been such a revealing experience to meet someone and right away be able to have conversations about things such as reincarnation and akashic records and astral travel -- topics considered by some to be akin to sixteenth-century witchcraft, she said. She talks about this stuff as if she knows what she is doing, or at least what she is talking about. She said she feels she is here because she has almost fulfilled her earthly incarnation cycle. She is hoping that after this life she may choose to do her work on the other side. She explained that her soul chose to incorporate at this time because a soul can make big advancement on Earth in times of great strife. If you choose to be aware that your thoughts and actions affect everything, then you know it is important to do the right thing every time in every moment. The big goal of humanity, she said, is the realization that we are all one, we must treat others as we want to be treated, and we must never turn away from another's pain. Whatever else that presents in life is just smoke and mirrors. It is how you choose to deal with the smoke and mirrors that defines you and your experience on Earth and moves your soul and fellow humans forward -- and by extension yourself as well, since we are all one. Life is a spiritual and a physical journey, and the two are intertwined at the most basic level. The value in life is in the journey, which is as full of surprises, pitfalls and rewards as any fantastic epic adventure. The goal is that we achieve Oneness, or Bliss, or whatever is at the end of one's personal rainbow. Basically at the end of the day and at the end of life, Bea said, you want to have a clean slate. Even better, if you want soul advancement, you have to take full responsibility for every single one of your actions and emotions, so the time is now to realize you have incorporated as a person for a greater goal and to try and advance the Oneness goal as well.

A lot to think about, and I have to say Bea does seem to live her philosophy. Bea is one of the most alive, joyful people I have ever met. I am grateful she persevered with me. I have decided to put one of her methods into effect immediately: say only positive things. She assured me that it is a wonderful tool that helps change the way you think. You begin constructing more positive thoughts in your head as well. I must start to look on the bright side of everything all the time. It sounds sickeningly sweet to me, but it works well for Beatrice.

As we reached the main area and were about to part, we met up with the two casually dressed military guys who had come to Civic Center in the first few days. They had come here to discuss the summit. They asked us for directions, which we gave, and then Beatrice began flirting lightly with them, keeping the conversation going with questions. They were telling us about DIA and how there are many people there and it is a very well organized operation and there is running water. Oh, my. That is when they told us there are several of these types of underground cities in safe locations around the country, and most of the elected leadership in the United States survived in these places. They call them hardened underground structures, and they are huge, self-sufficient structures, filled with military personnel of all branches and their families, elected leaders and their families and regular people of all kinds and their families.

What they were here to tell the group is that the government had heard our request to be a part of the summit, and the military guys were there to coordinate the convoy of people. They will begin flying people over as soon as tomorrow morning. They are welcoming as many people to the summit as want to show up, and if anyone wants to stay at DIA they are welcome. The special-ops people are getting the word out to as many people in as many places as they can before tomorrow. The government is coordinating transportation to make sure anyone and everyone can get there. It turns out the government has a big announcement to make to the people as well, so they welcome the attendance. I don't know if I even want to contemplate what the announcement could be about. I hope they are willing to contact the general and coordinate forces, or let him lead as long as he promises no violence. I would hope there would be strong participation by regular people moving forward; and there will have to be a voice for the people. Most importantly everything is going to be out in the open. No more leaders hiding away, issuing directives.

So I am off to the mess hall to get some food. Things are looking up, I think. After dinner and another town hall and the large group meditation tonight, the seven will gather for our small group meditation and a planning session for tomorrow. I don't know whether we will be joining the convoy or maybe flying on our own with Ian. I think we are also going to work with our group-energy exercises. I have not practiced telekinesis or anything like that, but I do find myself going to my meditation center for longer periods of time. I am feeling calm and relaxed even in the face of all of this chaos, so I will consider that a win.

11:06 p.m.

I think I understand more about why we were drawn together as a group of seven. There is something different about the energy we can generate together. Together we seem to be able to manipulate it. Our small-group energy is so different than what had been generated in the bigger groups at Civic Center or with the group here at Brush. That energy feels so much more generalized than what we create together. It begins when we stand in a circle and concentrate and then we somehow raise energy. It is like we have this very strong individual energy that we are able to merge into something that is stronger as a group.

Everyone is excited to be going to DIA and finally getting the ball rolling. Since we were all somewhat giddy, like teenagers before the big dance, we all wanted to play with the energy instead of doing the usual meditations. We started with a thought-forward exercise similar to the one Isolde did with the bullet. We stoked the group energy like a fire, and then directed the energy to one person. That person gathered the energy and would use it to form an image. I could not make something appear out of nothing, so I focused on a table across the room and for a brief moment it looked like an old stone wall. It was not a huge image but it was a big breakthrough moment for me. I had never been one to believe in anything but science. Until tonight when I created the stone wall, there was something I was not quite getting about being in and using the energy. Once I felt the group energy hum and felt that intense focus directed at me, I could feel an organic buzz in my very cells and in the air around me, and something in me believed I could tap it and be in it and then direct it. When I actually did it, it was a turning point, like a merging of the belief that all of this is organic science. It was one thing when I saw Isolde and Ian, and knowing they could do it contributed to my being able to. But the thought that I am psychic and can actually project energy, when assisted, and make it a form blows me away. I guess everyone is psychic to a certain degree, since being "psychic" just means someone who is better able to control the energy in existence all around us. The turning point is the belief that we can manipulate energy, I think. For me, the possibilities for this feel endless. I will be practicing this on my own.

We are going to fly to DIA tomorrow morning in the cargo plane with Ian as a group. The military planes will start arriving from DIA early tomorrow and will go until everyone who wants to go has been picked up. They sent the special-ops people far and wide with the message. They will be using vehicles and planes to ferry people from Denver and surrounding areas out to DIA. It feels good to have quick cooperation from the government and a plan in place. Everyone's spirits are lifted.

And everyone is talking about the warm running water for a shower.

For now, I am relaxing in my tent, trying to take it all in. I am not going to dwell on why the government made the decisions it did before the reversal. I do understand that mass chaos could have reined if the world had been informed of what might really be on the way. I am sure there were casualty studies that showed that letting people weather the storm as best they could would be better than telling everyone around the world and having the crazies take over and produce mass destruction, chaos and loss of life. What would we have thought if suddenly the military began showing up at people's doors, telling us the world was going to crack apart so we were going to have to drill like the military for a few months until it happened and then go to pre-assigned places once it did. I am sure many experts studied this from every angle. I just want more unification moving forward. I don't want someone else deciding my fate and then telling me what it is going to be. I know Reginald is struggling with the seeming lack of justice in this whole operation. He despises injustice of any kind. Of the entire group, he and I are most similar and we tend to gravitate toward one another when we get together as a group. Now our minds seem more in sync somehow. I can feel the edge of his thoughts, and he is really disturbed and determined to make a difference. Every single person should have a voice. I am also looking forward to seeing the setup at DIA.

We are not going to do any group meditation tomorrow

morning. I think everyone is just ready to get up and go. We are planning on leaving just after 7 a.m. DIA will have ambassadors in place to greet and show everyone around and get them settled and comfortable. Isolde and Bea are planning on setting up a group meditation at DIA for anyone who wants to participate after the summit. I know they will spend their time organizing that tomorrow. Everyone seems to have something they want to do there. My goal is to find the other doctors so I can talk shop and share this speed-healing theory of mine. I want to see if any of them would be game to try to do a doctor-type meditation. I don't know if I could lead something like that, but I would love to try.

From there, I think I will try to make my way home instead of over to the East Coast. It sounds as if DIA might be pretty well organized. If things go well and leadership is able to negotiate with the general and then the branches of service can be called out, things should move at a quick pace, at least with the clearing. I am hoping to stay at DIA until I can safely make my way to South Park. Or maybe I can help with clearing farther up the roads into the mountains, if that is what is needed. So I will spend the rest of my evening repacking the pack, hopefully for the last time, and then doing a mind reach to Mark. I like to link up to his mind and tell him about my day and send him pictures. I wonder if he will be able to feel my mind checking in and my excitement. I wonder if he can feel that I am alive and fine. I like to think so.

Day 8 5:46 a.m.

I don't feel like I slept. Everyone is excited and there was a lot of stirring around last night. I tossed and turned and must have drifted off, but it was not a restful endeavor. I am going to have another cup of coffee here behind my counter and then head over to the hangar where the cargo plane is waiting and the group will be meeting to fly over to DIA. The special-ops people will be arriving soon to take everyone else. We got more people last night who came in wanting to go to DIA from Brush. They said the word is going around. They met others on the road who knew of the summits. I don't know whether the Eastern and Western summits are going to have regular people involved or just leaders leading.

The horrible part of me wonders about the leaders of the states that are now gone. Do they still have a vote? It is starting to seem ridiculous to me that we are going to rebuild the same system. I don't want that degree of representative government going back into place. It will not be the right option moving forward. I will have to give more thought today about what an ordinary someone like me would want in place. I love how we all worked together at Civic Center and everyone showed up to the Town Hall because they wanted to. We moved them along pretty fast and got to the fun stuff. I know there has to be something like that we can do as a people to run our own regions. Government is not my specialty. I just want to go back to healing people. Let me amend that: I want to move toward guiding people to heal themselves.

Here I go about to roll up the camp again. Chaos has taken on a certain normalcy. I am looking so forward to getting back to civilization. I know there will be a time in my dotage that I tell the stories of this time. We are not the first civilization to rise and fall, and my story will be just another yawn for the young folks.

This cup of coffee has perked me right up. I am sure they have coffee at DIA. I know I should use this as an opportunity to give up some of my vices, but I really love coffee. I hope I am not picturing DIA as something it is not, but I have high hopes. I should take this time to chronicle some of the other stories I have heard but there are a few people I want to say goodbye to in case we lose one another in the shuffle of the transfer out to DIA so I am going to head out instead of doing any more journaling.

1:01 p.m.

DIA is beyond anything I could ever have imagined. I see now why they had to have ambassadors meet people coming in. It truly is a mammoth, self-sustained city, sprawling down underground six levels with a spring-fed reservoir, air-filtration systems, football-field sized fields of crops growing, live animals, two medical clinics, and everything one might have used in a city available here. Outside, there are extensive grounds and gardens in place growing root vegetables and other foods. I never even suspected any of it existed when I used to travel in or out of this airport.

I could go on and on about DIA, and I will if I get a chance later. It is endlessly fascinating. There are so many things I want to write about. A fascinating conversation Reginald and I had at the hangar this morning before we left. There is a family here from California that Ian and Isolde seem to know well, so I might finally learn more about them.

But I must first write about the military convoy and the fact that the military is using the mind link. I was at the hangar while Jon and Ian were getting everything ready to fly out early this morning. Reginald showed up, and then the military people from DIA came to get the convoy ready. The military are all casually dressed so that they distinguish themselves from the camo group, and also because they prefer it, I think. They were coordinating how the planes were going to fly in and out on the one runway, and were setting up a battery-powered machine to pull fuel from the ground. Some of them were setting up what looked like temporary relay stations. What I happened to notice as I watched them was how little verbal communication there seemed to be. I knew they had probably gotten everything planned before they showed up, but they were working together and I began to see signs of the mind sync whether they knew they were doing it or not. But then I realized they had to know they were actively using it. I wondered if they had been practicing or if small pockets of them happened on it and developed it or were

89

better at it than others, much like our group of seven. I wondered if it developed naturally because they knew one another and had worked together for a long time, or if the military had been developing it in an organized fashion. I know from experience how close one can feel to others in these incredible circumstances, which seem to help facilitate the mind link. Having companionable energy is a big part of the group strength, so it is easy to see that military personnel could fall easily into it if they live and work together and are willing to connect with one another. All these things began racing through my mind and prompted the fascinating conversation with Reginald.

We had been standing near one another after our initial greeting. Neither of us ever engages in small talk, so we were both staring out at the field when the convoy activity started up. I noticed the mind link happening among the military and began to watch in fascination. I could feel Reginald's mind at the outer edge of my own in that way we have developed. After a few minutes, I asked out loud if he was noticing what I was noticing in that they seemed to be able to coordinate this big effort pretty well in a strange environment without much talking going on. I did not see anyone wandering around aimlessly; everyone was moving purposefully from task to task without direction and things were getting set up quickly. Reginald agreed that there was something out of the ordinary happening. He told me he had been in the military, in special ops, and because of that he could basically follow what was going on out there. They were actively using the mind link, he said, because he was able to tap the outer edge of their energy flow and follow some of their directives with his mind.

He told me he was still in the National Guard and his family has a long history of service in the military, and that he feels the military still has the capacity to provide loyal service to the greater good. He had gotten a communication to go to DIA in his capacity as a military person in case of catastrophe, but had chosen not to go because that was not part of the greater good to him. He told me that he joined the group of seven primarily because his children are on the East Coast and he wants to get to them as soon as possible but he would step up and help where he felt it would make the most difference on the way. He and his wife were separated and she was with her parents and their children on the East Coast when disaster struck. He had spoken to them on the day of meltdown and he feels that they are safe. I could feel the hurt spot in him. Then he told me he knows of the general and would consider joining up with him if he had the best plan. He wants to make sure we all get the full picture from now on and considers it part of his personal mission to help keep everything out in the open.

Soon, the rest of our little group showed up to the hangar and we left for DIA. It was a quick flight and no one talked much. Isolde mentioned she hoped for one last small group gathering after the summit tonight, and I was glad I would get the chance to say goodbye to everyone. I was absorbed in my own thoughts about what Reginald had told me and the fact that the special-ops people were also working with the mind sync. I also was half-planning my return to South Park.

The ground around DIA is clear. I forgot what a large amount of land there is surrounding the airport. We were the only plane in the air and flew low to the ground. The land is furrowed and it is still raining, so there is a pall over the environment. The runways are all intact and free of debris. We taxied to a prearranged location and were met by a group of four ambassadors. I wondered why they sent four people, and also thought to myself, "If they have enough people here to send four people out to greet seven, how many people are actually here?" They led us into a room that was set up like a comfortable living room, and we all sat down as if for tea. They did serve water, but no food. They told us a little about the setup at DIA and how things were run. They asked what we wanted to do at DIA and where we wanted to stay. Once they found out what each of us wanted to do with our time, they let us know they could show us to our temporary lodging and then to whatever part of the airport we had indicated would most interest us. They suggested we sign up for a facility tour that lasts an hour and a half.

The whole process of intake of new people is in place and running smoothly. This was not a scrambled-together effort that is still evolving, as we had at Civic Center. My understanding is that there are small, neighborhood-like sectors, and there is still plenty of room because this place is enormous. DIA seems barely touched by this event. It has always had a futuristic feel to it, as all airports tend to do. But it seems the disaster was barely a blip on the radar here physically. The structure is still fully intact. I am going to sign up for that tour for sure. It goes underground to all of the levels.

I was curious to know about the four ambassadors, if they were in the military and how they had ended up at DIA. They were four civilians, one happened to be a military spouse. One was a younger, hipster guy who became my and Reginald's guide. I wanted to know his complete story and how he came to DIA, so he told us as we walked. He was unemployed when he moved to Denver and was reading an alternative newspaper at the coffee shop one day. He saw a full-page advertisement for a free three-day seminar on disaster preparedness. It was being put on by an arm of the city government through the transportation division. When he found out that snacks and water would be provided all three days, he signed right up. It was three days packed full of information. It began with the basics, such as how to administer cardiopulmonary resuscitation and first aid, how to tie a few knots and keep yourself warm with little clothing, and progressed all the way to how to save yourself and others if buried alive and how to survive off your body fat if you are stuck with no food.

Included in the three days was a brief seminar about alternate routes that could be taken if traditional routes were blocked, and the focus seemed to be on which train tracks should be followed to DIA from just about anywhere in the city. He said it was a fascinating seminar and he had gotten so much valuable information he could not believe more people had not signed up for it. He left with a clear message that DIA was a safe location and a good place to head in case of disaster. As a new resident of

Denver, he dined out on the story of the seminar and disaster preparedness, and in that way told others how to be ready.

After he had taken the seminar, he said, he started noticing other little things the government seemed to be doing to get people to think about a big disaster and to prepare for something to happen. He told me a lot of his friends were into the zombie-revolution theory and the Department of Homeland Security played right into it, putting out a zombie warning on its website with links to disaster-preparedness blurbs. It was done tongue in cheek but was supposed to get people talking about what they would do or how ready they were if disaster struck.

He said he had not had to take advantage of any extreme methods to get here; he made it to the airport in his car the morning everything started happening after contacting everyone he knew by every social media outlet he knew and urging them to do the same thing. He was not surprised when he got here to find organization in place, and fell right into the organization effort. They welcomed anyone and everyone that came that day, and any time afterward. They helped get the stranded travelers settled. Many airport employees had also come with their families, and they really know their way around.

Then there is the disaster staff, a fairly large group of people that was put in place to ready the ship, man it through the storm and make sure it was up and running quickly and a safe harbor for the leaders and others who are here. The disaster-preparedness staff, a small crew initially, worked in secret in underground locations from the time the airport was being built. They designed the infrastructure and then slowly hired the rest of the large disaster staff. The airport was so big and the planning so extensive that the staff who worked on the disaster side of things never realized how big their department was getting. Each worker would go to his or her individual location in the extensive labyrinth, on whatever level, and never realized preparedness was happening on a large scale all over the airport.

So they have everything here. I am loving the running water, powered by solar, wind and garbage. It is not like the old running water, but it is amazing to have it again to wash hands and look forward to a full-body shower. There seem to be huge stockpiles of everything in addition to growing food, live animals, and water and air filtration. It is not being run by the military as one might think. The disaster staff and their families are in place until such time as they get governmental orders. Their salary was paid by the federal government. Things are running smoothly, and the directive in place is to hold steady on course. People are happy to have such organization in place here in the face of chaos out in the world. Everyone looks for things to help with, pitches in and volunteers where needed. There is quite a spirit of cooperation in place here.

There is a central gathering place here large enough to hold every single person here and more, and we will meet there tonight for the summit. Everyone is happy that the leaders finally are coming into the open. It felt as though there was danger they were avoiding but did not mind that we faced -- or that there might be something else coming that they know about that we do not.

The general and his militia have not yet made contact, so I figure they are still underground, waiting for all their members to gather. It will be interesting to see what happens.

Ian and Isolde asked one of the four DIA ambassadors if a family they knew had made it in from California. One of the ambassadors was staying near the family, and Ian and Isolde headed to that sector to stay the night there. Beatrice took off for the agricultural section to see the herb gardens. Philip and Jon headed over to the solar facility. Reginald and I both wanted to go straight to the map room to check the areas that have been surveyed from the air. We wanted to make sure our loved ones are indeed in safe geographical locations. Both of us got lucky, and both families are in the solid regions, not those very large sections colored blue to indicate water. Until I saw that map, the changes to the continent were hazy. Now I realize how fragmented and covered with water our continent has become.

Reginald and I both chose a single room, and the

ambassador showed us to our residence hall. The singles residences are off a long narrow hallway with a door every five feet leading to a compact space that reminds me of a room on a cruise ship, but even smaller. It is a luxury to be in my own room with the ability to wash my hands and use a regular toilet. There are no locks or keys for any of the doors, but our guide said he has not heard of a single theft so far. I could almost feel him waiting for the questions. I think he was mind-reaching Reginald and me, but it felt like a little moth fluttering against glass.

I immediately dropped my backpack on the bed, changed into a dry pair of socks and, out of habit, started writing my impressions in my journal so I don't forget.

I want to get my bearings and get a feel for the place before I do anything else, which is why I want to take the facility tour immediately. There is a tour leaving every three hours because they are processing so many people into the airport every day.

After the tour I plan to visit one of several mess halls. The ambassador said we can go into any one of them and get a variety of hot food. He was not implying it is like a Vegas buffet, but there is food from many cultures here and it is readily available.

We can begin volunteering or learning if, when and where we like. It is encouraged but not required. They have every level of school set up, and there are training programs for those who want to explore different fields. It is a neat environment that seems to foster cooperation. It is nice to see so many multi-cultural faces and be among so many people again. Everyone is abuzz with talk of the summits, which begin at five.

I am curious to meet the people Ian and Isolde know from California, and maybe learn a little more about them and their family there. And I am looking very much forward to the summit and finally getting everything out on the table. I love my little room for the convenience and privacy. It is designed well for a small space. It is nice to feel settled and like I am back in civilization.

Once the ambassador leading the tour began to open up

and speak, I was able to delve right into all his thoughts and emotions while he was showing us around and answering our questions. I got verbal answers and a lot more from him. I know Reginald was able to get a read on him as well, because I could feel his mind there. I am sure our ambassador was surprised at how few questions we had at the end of the tour.

11:06 p.m.

I thought my mind had reached a plateau for unreality until tonight. Now it is as if my world went "tilt" again.

The big announcement is that a huge new continent has arisen. Flyovers indicate it extends up and down the East Coast of the United States, stretches across the Atlantic, and up and down the coast of Africa on one side and South America on the other side. It is an enormous island continent.

After the government made the big announcement, there was a sham summit and we the people effectively fired our leaders here, a.k.a. the Mid Regional Government.

I also found out more about Ian and Isolde and their family. The family they asked about when they arrived is the family of their house manager, Maria, who helped raise them. The families are intertwined as Maria and Mimi, Ian and Isolde's grandmother, together helped raise the twins and their siblings and Consuela, who is Maria's daughter, three months older than Ian and Isolde who might as well have been the triplet since she was so close in age and raised so closely. They all grew up together in huge houses across the world.

It has been a fascinating night. I don't even know how my hand is steady enough to write. I feel drained and ebullient at the same time. I will start at the beginning, at the sham summit.

All the leaders sat out in the open on a raised platform in one of the larger auditoriums. The platform brought them above the first five or so rows of seating, so they were above or at eye level with most of the crowd. Their chairs were arranged in a large

U behind a podium, facing the stands, and they were already seated when we were ushered in. The room is large enough to accommodate many, many people, but large sections were cordoned off, so we were all funneled into a tight little section right in front of them. It ran through my mind that they did not want us to be comfortable and stay longer than necessary, or they did not trust us and wanted to keep an eye on us. They did make it a point to be out in the open with no Secret Service, but the setup still felt separatist and elitist with the way we were brought in and the way the platform was raised and facing us across a gap. It looked more like there was going to be a stage play than a national summit.

The summit began with a very moving speech from a governor who has nothing left to govern. The head of facility at DIA then reassured everyone that we have plenty of stockpiled supplies. Plenty of seeds of every variety in storage and ready to go, and active crops doing well now. Water and air filtration systems working well even without the solar portion of the operation. We will not have any shortages in the near future and are well prepared for anything, he said. Everything is right and tight at DIA.

The Speaker of the House let us know that we still have not heard from the general but that the populace is secure and that rebuilding efforts will soon be under way and the military will be called out to help organize. It will be our strength as a people that sees us through these hard times, the Speaker said. It felt a little late for that speech. There has really been no sign of the leaders out and about, so I wondered how they could know how hard it has been or how hard it will be in places such as Civic Center and the neighborhoods. They will probably stay at facilities such as DIA, which were readied and barely shook during the upheaval, so it is not a crisis they faced or are facing directly.

Then the Speaker made the big announcement. A huge new island continent has risen and it borders three and maybe four continents. He went on to say they have been doing flyovers and will be exploring on the ground soon and are excited that a huge new land has emerged.

The Speaker then informed us the leaders would openly discuss some pertinent issues relating to this discovery as well as what is going on with the general and his group, and then vote on how to proceed. Tomorrow, the leadership of the three summits would get on the field radio, compare notes and take a big vote. It looked as though it was going to be business as usual, and they were going to go through the motions as if we the people had just stopped by Congress that day to be spectators in the gallery. They had probably already decided everything, and this really was just a play to them.

The entire event did feel orchestrated. Butter us up with heartwarming speeches, announce that we are looking good, and everyone will be comfortable and feel free to grow complacent. We will have everything we need for the immediate and long term. Once everyone is feeling good and a little antsy from the speeches, roll out the huge issues, gloss 'em over, and then the few will decide how the majority will proceed without even asking an opinion. I guess the people were supposed to be just onlookers to this summit.

That is when Reginald strode to the platform. None of us has our weapons, since weapons are not allowed in the airport, so everyone knew he was not going to shoot up the room or something. But he is big, he was really worked up, and he was moving fast. The Secret Service agents all ran up to the dais but you could hear Reginald's huge voice from corner to corner.

"I mean these people no harm," he roared. "Let me have my say here."

All eyes were riveted. He climbed the side stairs to the platform and faced the leaders from the podium.

"I don't want decisions being made for me anymore," he said. "I do not need to be led. From here I want to be a group of people making decisions together and moving forward. Every single person who wants a vote about how to proceed on everything from how we get services going again to what kind of government goes in place here and on a new continent should get a vote. So I think your job as our elected leaders from here on out should be collectors and distributors of information. Hop down off this dais, become one of the people and compile every little detail and bit of information you can think of about anything pertinent so you can spread the information. Every person should get a chance to talk about this new continent and other issues in their own languages and on their time, and then together as a people I feel sure we can address the issues from every angle and form a smart plan."

"We had a little thing called Town Hall we got going when there were no leaders around. I think we could put that in place instead of this. And from here on out, let's give everyone the whole picture."

Reginald then turned to us who had been sitting riveted in the stands and said, "The general and his militia are currently camped on the new continent. Our executive leadership wants to send a large military force over. Let us try to form a plan for peace as we rebuild the world."

He asked for a show of hands if everything he had said was acceptable to those of us in the stands. There was an overwhelming cheer. "Then let us convene here tomorrow morning when we will ALL (his voice can really roar) have decided on how we will proceed and THEN we make contact on the field radio to let them know of OUR decisions."

He turned back and thanked those on the platform for their service to the people and welcomed them to the general populace. He let them know they should convey to the other regional summits that we the people would like a say and a vote on anything and everything that might concern us as a nation from here on out. He then turned back to the stands to address the crowd once more, saying he does not want to be a leader and to be careful of anyone too eager to jump in and fill that role. He is a proud member of the Guard and will be more than happy to step up when the call is issued. His personal desire, he said, is to get to the East Coast as soon as possible to be with his loved ones.

Then he stepped down and left the room.

The Speaker tried to gain control of the room, but no one wanted to pay attention to him and the din of conversation overwhelmed the effort. Reginald was right. There are some huge issues on the table here, and there will be far-flung repercussions to decisions made tonight and in the next few days. There are too few of us left to think we cannot be consulted and have a place in the decision making. I think leadership probably already had a plan in place for how they wanted to proceed, but it is really we as a people who need to decide.

Finally, the leadership dispersed off the dais and everyone was still talking loudly when Ian, Isolde and Consuela climbed the stairs to the platform. The action caught everyone's attention, so the room quieted a little. The trio began to sing, and clearly they have been harmonizing together for a very long time. They were really good, and sang a medley of show tunes. When the large room had quieted almost completely, they stopped singing and Ian said to the stands, "We should sing some songs soon." The juxtaposition of the huge announcement and dismissal of the government against the amazing a capella singing, followed by the somewhat ridiculous suggestion that everyone sing together, created complete quiet in the room and all focus on the platform. Into the silence Isolde suggested that the meditation move forward. The crowd was not sold and began stirring again. Isolde began repeating the suggestion in several languages, and I saw Beatrice walking up the stairs to the platform to stand behind her. Then I saw Philip and Jon make it up there. I felt drawn to support Isolde, so I headed to the front of the room and onto the platform. I could feel the energy zeroing in on us with curiosity and quieting again as we all concentrated on Isolde. Our group mind link is strong, and I think the crowd could feel it as we all focused on one another and together built our energy hum. Led by Isolde, we sent out waves of calm to the crowd. Isolde reassured everyone in six languages that we make better decisions when we come from a place of peace and tranquility. She said she is not trying to lead either; she just wants a group meditation for peace. Meditation is non-denominational and brings each individual to his or her center. Everyone wants peace.

I felt the energy of the crowd zoning in on the peace theme, and they finally quieted and Isolde led a really strong group meditation. It went beautifully, possibly the most powerful group meditation yet.

Isolde did not try to hold the crowd after the meditation. She gave the usual instructions to "remember to center and let all your actions and reactions come from a place of forgiveness." She said these are exciting times and it is easy to get worked up, but it is important that we take time to be grateful to be together and to be a part of this pivotal time in history. "Let us all work together to make wise decisions and try to be aware of the bigger picture so together we can create goodness. We have a lot to do, so let us begin listing each task that needs to happen. The list will be even longer than a greedy child's Christmas list, I am sure." This drew a laugh. "Come up with solutions for everything from how you think the government should be run to how you think we can bring services back on line for the masses. I know the fine minds among us together can come up with a satisfactory plan."

Then she walked down off the platform and we all followed. Our small band made our way to Consuela's and Maria's largish family apartment for a quick planning session. The unit is a decent size but feels as if it is bursting at the seams now that Ian and Isolde have parked their gear in the living room -- "for now," they say -- and invited people over. I am sure it feels good for them to be around family again and be able to let their hair down.

When the place began to feel crowded to me, I volunteered to go get Reginald because we did not know if he would want to find us or if he would know where to find us. He and I were staying near one another and I wanted to use the walk over to compose my thoughts, which were roiling.

As I walked along, it struck me that we had just fired our regional government, which is a scary precedent. The most powerful tool the leaders have is the power to call out the branches of service and the ability to allocate our resources, and it is the people who vest them with that power so it is our decision as to whether we want to vest those same people with decision making in this new environment. Maybe we want no leaders at all. I don't think this current set of elected leadership will know how to run things peacefully on a new continent between several different countries and cultures. Just the opposite would be true, I think. Our foreign policy was nothing to be proud of, nor was the foreign policy of many other supposedly civilized countries, so I want to do something different this time around, not the same stuff that wasn't working. I like the idea of a Town Hall format so everyone, all the regular people, have a voice and not one person's opinion slips through the cracks. Why do we need representative government at this point? Why do we need leaders who want to do things the same old way in the face of all of this new energy?

I was thinking of the general and his band being on the new continent. I wondered why they would not want us to know he was there. I did not think it would be a good idea to call the regular military out to go and meet him on another continent for a struggle for the new land, when our own land is going to need every pair of hands to clear and rebuild our own country. But I also thought we can't be the only country to have spotted this new land mass and probably want it for our own. It borders at least two other continents, maybe three. Do we want this general over there representing us to other countries that might show up? What if he uses violence to pursue his agenda? I don't want there to be one life lost on this new continent over any of this, American or otherwise. I don't want to involve our military in a world war with another country over the new land. I don't want a new continent so close to the United States being taken over by a country whose system I disagree with either. Selfishly, I was wondering where all this would leave me. Down to my core, I was missing Mark. I was grateful to have my small group, but I really just wanted to be with him and the babies, far away from this place. Reginald was feeling the same thing, so we were good company. I greeted him and he said hello and then he just stepped out of his room and pulled his door closed behind him and we turned in sync and began walking. I was again glad we could walk along together without having to make conversation. I wanted to keep my thoughts to myself and he did too.

The atmosphere at the family apartment was convivial. No one seemed at all disturbed about the fact that we did not have a working government in place to address any issues and that there seems to be a rogue militia representing our interests on a new continent. We all crowded in the living room and dining room to come up with our plan for what we felt we needed to accomplish this evening. It was Philip's suggestion to have everyone here in the room and anyone here at DIA to write down the one issue at the forefront of their minds. Add a suggestion about how to get it resolved if you can think of one, he said, and drop it in the drop box he will create. After compiling concerns and suggestions for solutions, we hopefully can move on to a planning stage to get the concerns addressed. I am sure the concerns will be fairly general across the board, but this encourages even the smallest detail to come to light.

Philip said he would establish a central drop point for the ideas and suggestions, and once it felt like everyone had turned in what they would, he would compile the ideas and write out what everyone wanted to talk about, put it on a clipboard and bring it back to the people where we could gather again in the auditorium and do the town hall where anyone could discuss any issue. We would put the one-minute time limit on the speaking, since there were so many issues and so many things people would feel strongly about. Then, if the issue became too complicated or heated, we could table it for future discussion. We could decide together what needed votes immediately, in the short term and in the long term. There are some brilliant minds and amazing people here at the airport. I bet we will see resolutions to the issues pretty quickly if we work together. We all agreed this sounded like a great plan. Philip had his task and off he went, and I knew he intended to go get Sara to help him get it all set up. They had been inseparable since Brush.

Ian, Isolde, Consuela and the family planned to go out

among the people and volunteer their services as interpreters. Jon was headed toward the tech wing, to be ready to help implement any practical solutions quickly. Beatrice wanted to find and talk with the military guys that had come to Brush, saying she wanted to get their opinion on what they think about all this from a military perspective. Reginald decided to go find some fellow attorneys to intimidate into coming up with a new legislative system. (Totally kidding about the intimidation part, but he is just so serious all the time, so focused on making it right.)

It took us about fifteen minutes to actually roll out the door, as is the way with a big family's leave taking. During that interval, Consuela read hesitation in my demeanor and invited me to tag along with her so we could talk medical science on the way to the main gathering areas. She had been doing stem-cell research before the world went upside down. She could feel my healing energy, she said, and knew I was a doctor. It struck me funny that she said that because when I had walked by the clinic today on the tour and saw the two people inside, I knew immediately they were doctors. I wondered briefly if one's profession gives off an energy. I agreed to walk with her, of course, because I could not think of a worse fate than braving a crowd by myself and having to make conversation with strangers. I had been slightly tempted to head back to my room and write. I was burning with curiosity about Consuela and Maria and how their family had become intertwined with Ian's and Isolde's, but I did not want to ask outright. Consuela, being almost as psychic as Beatrice, picked up on my curiosity and said she would tell me the story on our way over to the main gathering areas.

As we walked, Consuela told me she had gotten Maria's permission to tell the story of how Maria ended up in the United States from Argentina. She told me Maria had been a bright foreign-exchange student studying the sciences on a yearlong scholarship. She met a handsome fellow exchange student who was on a six-month program, and they spent the fall semester exploring their host country and falling in love. On his last night in the United States, the handsome student got a bottle of wine and seduced Maria. Maria found out four months later that she was pregnant. She had been so innocent that she did not know she was experiencing pregnancy symptoms. She had not heard from her lover and thought her symptoms had to do with sheer misery. She was humiliated and sick at heart. She was from a religious family and was too ashamed to tell them what had happened. She was alone and pregnant and her school term was coming to an end. She decided she would have the baby and give it up for adoption. She would tell her family she was attending summer school and would return in September rather than May as originally planned. Once the adoption was complete, she would go back to Argentina and do penance for the rest of her life.

She spent a miserable few months contemplating this choice. Immediately after the birth she realized there was no way she was giving up her baby.

Soon after Consuela was born, Maria responded to an ad Mimi had placed for household help. The ad said the position came with a small private room and bath. Maria doubted she would have a shot at the job because she would have to bring infant Consuela with her to the interview. Maria took the bus across town for the interview to a really nice neighborhood and then had to walk up a long hill and driveway to a large house. Mimi answered the door herself when Maria arrived. She was slim and had ramrod-straight posture. Her facial bone structure made her striking but not beautiful. She had light blue eyes that focused intently on whomever she was speaking with. She welcomed Maria into a beautiful room off the side of a grand staircase without ever mentioning the fact that Maria was carrying an infant and sweating profusely, with two circles of leaked milk on the front of her shirt. Mimi directed Maria to the washroom and told her she would be back in twenty minutes to conduct the interview. Maria almost cried with relief. The baby needed to be nursed, and she needed time to pull herself together. When Mimi returned twenty-five minutes later, she was carrying a tray with a plate of sandwiches, a pitcher of lemonade and two frosted glasses. Maria did cry then, and Mimi told her to pull herself together and eat because they had work to do.

As Maria ate Mimi described what she was looking for. She was in town helping her daughter, who was expecting twins. Her daughter and son-in-law were moving out of this house to a bigger one, both were juggling successful careers and neither had done a thing to prepare for a move or a birth. The job was a management position with no physical labor. Mimi needed help initially getting packers and movers to pack this place and unpack and set up the new place. The new home was much larger and needed a staff that would have to be hired. She said she was experiencing a bit of a language barrier with many of the applicants, so she would need Maria in that capacity initially as well. They would have to hire an au pair, a driver, a gardener, a cook and a full-time housekeeper.

After the twins were born, Mimi would devote herself to them for the first few months while her daughter and son-in-law continued to pursue their careers. Maria's job would be to manage the household and staff and make sure everything continued to operate smoothly for her daughter and son-in-law after Mimi had gone. Consuela could be with her at all times. Mimi would like to learn Spanish from Maria if she had time, and hoped Maria would speak to the twins always in Spanish. Mimi planned to speak to them only in French. All of this was said in a straightforward, businesslike manner. Then Mimi named an extraordinary salary, which caused Maria to ask if she had to pay for the room. Mimi looked her in the eye and said, "The ad said the room was included. I will never be dishonest with you and I will expect the same of you in return. You don't strike me as a liar or a cheat. I can't abide either. I want you to be comfortable and maybe even happy here, and create a nice environment. I don't care what brought you, but I get a feeling that you and I will be able to work together to achieve my goals. Do you want the job?"

That was Mimi in a nutshell, Consuela said. Mimi received strong first impressions, shot from the hip and never regretted a single decision. She was straightforward and honest, well-mannered and polite to a fault. Mimi's plan had been to get everything in place and running smoothly, help with the babies for a few months, and then head back to her small Southern hometown where she was the reigning queen. Then her banker husband had a heart attack and died right after the twins were born, and she ended up never leaving. Together, Mimi and Maria tended the home fires as the parents pursued their very successful careers and the family grew. Maria went back to school, finished her undergraduate work and then earned a master's degree. She devoted herself to Consuela and her adopted family.

When Isolde and Ian's parents got pregnant with their sixth child, they moved to an estate with extensive grounds. They sold Maria one of the bungalows with acreage on the property. Maria had long ago told her family about Consuela, and there had been many trips back and forth to Argentina. When the economy in Argentina took a dive, many of Maria's family moved to the States and settled nearby. They all grew up as a big, happy, convivial family. Mimi and Maria ran the household together, helped raise the children and grew to be great friends along the way. Consuela said both Maria and Mimi would always tell you the arm of friendship stretches out at odd times and in tough times for a reason.

When Consuela and I reached one of the main common areas, there were not as many people as I thought there would be out and about. I expected to see groups standing around discussing things and chattering excitedly. Instead, there were a few people going here or there, and there seemed to be tension in the air. I wondered what was going on. Clearly people were getting nervous about having fired the Mid Region government.

There also was a lack of organization, which always throws things into disarray. Since organization and attention to detail are among my strong suits, and in the spirit of getting things in the open and getting some talking points established, I suggested that we use Bea's bulletin-board idea and put some cork or white boards up around the common areas of DIA so that people could have a focal point to gather and talk about what should go up on

107

a list like this. To demonstrate what I was talking about, I pulled out some paper and wrote my suggestion. I wanted to get communications going right away, and my suggestion was that we build and launch a new satellite into space that is dedicated to cell phones that have been reprogrammed. Distribute the reprogrammed cell phones all over the country and make them accessible to everyone in a public location so calls can begin to go back and forth. I did not know if any of this would work in the face of the magnetic disruption, but one could hope. I thought after I wrote it out that maybe I should have put down something medicine related, but the selfish part of me won yet again. I called some people over and asked where I might find a bulletin board or white board. Thankfully, this started the conversation about what we were doing, and gave all of us something to do together and seemed to get some conversations going.

Consuela and I then went to track Jon down to see if he could put together bulletin boards, or even find some. We knew he would figure it out if we gave him the gist of what we wanted, a place where people could go to write out their idea of what needs to be addressed and then post it. People could wait around to see what was being posted or talk about what they felt were the issues we faced right away, in the short term and in the long term. As the list of concerns, wants, desires and issues grew, they could be taken from the common areas to Philip, who would be compiling the information at the central location. Once the list had been compiled and readied it could be taken to the auditorium for the town hall format we seem to be enacting everywhere we go. We needed to get people out and talking about these things with one another, not huddling in their living rooms, doubting what we had done.

I was beginning to get the feeling someone was going to have to help pull this large group together to do just that if we wanted the plan of not being led to stick. Although I had never wanted to be the one to pick up the torch and stand for this or that kind of thing, I thought, "Well, here I am in the thick of it," and I influenced the decision that helped bring us here so I should take action and speak for what I feel is right. I don't want to be someone who sits around and reacts to events anymore, I must do what I feel is right. And I felt what was right was to set my mind to organization and stand up and compel others to action.

I told Consuela we should walk the narrow halls of the singles quarters and then the family quarters to get people out and mingling and talking about the summit and issues. Consuela jumped aboard, and we went around shouting like town criers. "Bring out your issues!" People were hesitant until we began literally banging on doors. Consuela is like Bea in that she is vibrant and fun. She speaks who knows how many languages and would talk to anyone who opened a door after we had banged on it. She would shout things such as "Pizza delivery!" or "I have your newspaper subscription!" It sounded funnier in Japanese. People began to come out when they heard the noise and would fall into the line behind us. We got a parade feel going as we moved through the residence hallways. The crowd grew, and everyone took to banging on the doors. I finally was beginning to hear that lively chatter and conversation I had hoped for. We met up with Ian and Isolde, who took up the charge and headed off to other residence halls in other wings to do the banging on doors, bringing out the people.

We initially were directing people to Philip and Sara at the central gathering spot, but as the crowd got bigger and Jon got the other areas set up, people filtered there. The common areas drew small groups of people who were talking animatedly and even laughing.

Then came a most amazing sight. The leaders had come out and were mingling with the people. They were actually listening instead of trying to talk and lead and campaign. Their intermingling encouraged everyone else to talk to others outside their small groups, and I was so happy to see larger and more multicultural groups of people form and begin to flow into larger spaces such as the mess halls to continue their conversations. Things started to come together, and after a few hours Philip said the input of concerns and suggestions had gone from avalanche to trickle and the requests were all starting to look the same. He said there were some great ideas in the suggestion pile to work with, and that he thought we were ready to move on to the town hall. He said there were some great suggestions the scientists and fix-it guys could tackle.

I was curious and a bit nervous to see how the town hall would translate to such a large, mixed crowd who had been unexpectedly thrown together in a highly charged atmosphere. I am thrilled to write that it went smoothly. Everyone stuck to the one-minute limit. People were very respectful of listening to others. It was exciting to see so many people involved and hear so many great ideas and suggestions. Ian, Isolde, Consuela and plenty of other translators were available. We got a lot resolved and many other things had to be tabled. The main bulletin board will stay in place for new ideas.

The main issues seemed to be rebuilding, communication, travel and what our involvement on a new continent should be. Rebuilding is under way, so we can step that up. People wanted communication established as soon as possible and restoration of the ability to travel. Many said they would be interested in going to the new continent.

There were some great suggestions to go with the ideas. One was that cars already on the roads be fixed up and left there as transportation that could be used by anyone, and then left at their destination to be picked up and used by another, similar to the free bike program a European city had in place. It was suggested (I wonder by whom?) that nondenominational meditation spaces be set up all over the airport and anywhere else more than two people planned to settle. People were interested in exploring the new continent and maybe living there right away as long as there was no danger of being shot or taken over by a hostile government; they wanted total freedom for the new continent.

All the basics were covered. We need to rebuild such and such right away. Get running water and power up and running and all the roads cleared. Bury the dead. What to do about the general (nothing). Make regular contact with other countries every day with full disclosure of what we are doing and what our future plans are. Everything should be out in the open now, and we hope to set an example of peace right away. If we can get back on our feet before any other country does, we certainly will send relief. Another plan was to start building outward from the airport, using the airport as the hub. I don't know if there is going to be such a thing as private ownership of land in the aftermath. Who will own the new continent? Maybe it will be like a giant world land rush.

One of the many suggestions for peace was that we don't call out the military. They are free to volunteer, just like the rest of us. No one gets to make the call on another's life. So we dismissed the idea of calling out the military for anything. Why don't they get as much of a say as anyone else? I don't think we need a forceful approach or protecting. We need organization. The politicians said the other countries were in as bad or worse shape as America and had asked if we would be able to send aid. It is going to be the people for the people from here on out. Resources will still have to be carefully managed and allocated, but the town hall tonight has shown us this can be done effectively. The people are in place who have organized it all along and can show others the system. Now that we are all invested personally, not just because someone else forced us to do something, things will get accomplished -- and they will be accomplished with a willing and happy heart. Special ops will continue to operate in their developed roles until those too can be tapered off and they can be released.

Another idea for peace was that we send volunteer ambassadors to the new continent. They could set up in the white tent of peace, with white flags flying, and show other countries that we will settle side by side peacefully with anyone from any country. Let us make the new continent something special in history: people from many countries coming together to live in peace and maybe self-government. Contact the other nations of the world and see if they agree with that strategy. Let us also see if their people want a say in how things on the new continent are going to progress. If not, their people are told of this new continent and the leaders can let us shuttle as many of their people who want to leave to the new continent or to America.

We have to let other countries know that the heavily armed general and his militia are on the new continent, and that they are not representative of what we stand for or what we want. We don't know if leadership has shared that news with other countries. Or maybe they want him out there to draw fire. Who knows?

There was something about every mind being tuned into the group welfare in that auditorium. It was energetic and the field was fertile. There were some great ideas about how we want to be governed. Even the children got a voice. They had ideas and some great things to say. They also had some silly suggestions, which everyone tried to consider with a straight face as they were explained. There were light moments and heavy moments, but I think we made it through the issues faster than the House or Senate could have.

Initially, we decided, leaders or representatives will be chosen by lottery. The names of everyone who is interested will go into a hat to be chosen. The responsibility of the representatives will be liaisons and deliverers of information. They will be true representatives of the people in that they vote as the majority of their people voted. As with jury duty, if you get the call, you are being pressed into civic responsibility you volunteered for and may have to set other things aside to step up. We are social animals and groups are our natural environment, so civic responsibility should continue so that the society can thrive. Civic responsibility breeds cooperation and working together, and that is how we got this far. I am sure if we take that up a notch, it is the same kind of thing that takes us to the next level and the next, whatever those may be. I know somehow we have to come up with this as a people and a group for everyone to be committed to having this cooperation idea to stick. After the town hall, we were feeling a wonderful group energy. I could feel it in the air. Everyone was still pretty juked up and spilled out into the common areas, talking animatedly. It was wonderful to hear different languages being spoken. Multicultural groups were discussing different ways of government in different countries and how to implement the best of all the old systems.

Transportation to the east and west coasts will be scheduled immediately and hopefully to other countries in the near future. A lottery will determine who gets to be the first going anywhere. All streets are to be cleared and repaired for use as travel thoroughfares beginning with the main streets and ending up at the least used, working on the infrastructure for water as the streets are fixed. Communication has to be tabled, since there are no immediate solutions other than the "mail room," a small room set up for letters travelling back and forth. Sadly, there have been very few. There were great ideas though, so I am hopeful. We contacted other countries and everyone has agreed their focus is on their own people and that they are hoping the new continent is one where people from all countries can live in peace. We let other countries know the Mid Region is in no way affiliated with the general and that we support only peaceful resolution to any situation.

After the town hall, our little group held a brief meeting and decided we would meet tomorrow morning at Consuela's and Maria's to do a small group meditation to see if we can employ the group energy to do some telekinesis. If someone would have told me three months ago that I would be actively participating in some extra-sensory perception, I would have laughed outright at the absurdity. There's the sci-fi element again, but I cannot deny that it is real. When I think of its use in the future, I think of the kids who are probably already working with the new energy at places like the airport where strong friendships are being forged, and I know they won't remember a time without this lightened energy. The energy is becoming a part of whom and what they are, just as it is for me. ESP probably is the next wireless phone or Internet, and the children who will be growing up in these times will laugh when they think of our generation struggling without it, like cave people trying to communicate verbally and with hand gestures and written symbols.

All over the world, people are coming together, organizing and hopefully realizing that ESP is here to stay. If Ian and Isolde can move a little child's ball around with just the force of their linked energy, what might we be able to put together as a group of seven, or the military as a huge group? That begs the question of how they would use it.

We want to be out early after our small group meditation and get a read on the crowd. There is someone from the town hall monitoring governmental communication on the field radio at all times now, and we are curious to know if the other leaders are going to just ignore what we have done here or if they will bow to what we feel is the inevitable. We wonder what the rest of the world is going to think of this. We are hoping they pick it up as an example. People are the world's best resource. It is time to begin educating instead of repressing large groups of people. It is dangerous to have one person or a few people in power above all others. We know the leaders of the Eastern and Western regions are probably discussing it among themselves, but they can't ask the leaders who were at the Mid Regional directly what happened. We explained to them that this is not a rebellion or hostile takeover. It is time to make a change, and we voted on it as a people. It is people who give leaders legitimacy, just as we give legitimacy to certain pieces of paper and call it money. We know it is just paper but we print it to regulate it and exchange it and give it all sorts of power. At the end of the day it is still just paper we have invested with extreme power, and at the end of the day leaders are just people making decisions.

I don't want to be led by the nose anymore and fed partial information about what is going on in the world. I want to know where we are going, and then why and when. I want to be a part of a good system that I love and love participating in. I want to talk things out among my peers and have many minds come up with solutions to the problems that affect us directly together. I don't want to turn that power over to anyone else ever again.

The world has grown too small to go about this any other way for now. We can decide about the future when we get there. We have proved in these microcosms at Civic Center and DIA that rule by the people can work at this point. In return, I will try to put myself out there more and be part of the group. Civic responsibility and civic pride will be part of my makeup, and I will instill it in my children. I won't just be a spectator at the sport from here on out. It is time to step up and play. I will work with anyone I can on this new energy because I think it will pave the way to a harmonious future.

I think Reginald has a point: Recruit only those to lead who do not want to lead. Those who despise leadership will be the best organizers because they cannot stand to boss others around. I would use myself as an example. I don't necessarily like to lead, but I really don't like to be led. That's one of the many reasons I became a doctor instead of simply being in healthcare, but I thought the doctor-nurse roles were outdated. Instead of making the relationship between the doctors and nurses a team that would utilize everyone's expertise, there was a doctor "in charge," and nurses, who had much more practical experience could not challenge a diagnosis or speak up about a viable treatment plan. In the end it would have been the patient who benefitted if things would have been different.

Those are the types of things that have to change from the top down. No more narrow leadership where there is only one perspective. Perhaps a cooperative based on specialization, with education being the foundation of our new system. What if every kid spoke six languages? What a small world it would be if people were allowed to travel to other countries for free and sit around in public places, debating issues in a friendly way with the people of that country and getting everything resolved for the good of everyone by talking things through.

A couple of large groups are flying to Western and Eastern regional summit locations tomorrow or the next day. We decided we have to have representatives of the people showing other regular people what happened here and how to do a town hall of their own before executive leadership tries to steamroll what we have done. We should give everyone the chance to stand up and have a say about anything they want and then get to help shape the decision-making. Representative government only works with a non-educated populace. We had outgrown the system. People are too smart these days, and communication was too good, and the world had grown too small to keep that musty old system in place. We as a people should have stepped up to change things, but I know I was too comfortable in my world to really care, as were many. I did not care that the system had become so convoluted. I could barely even figure out how to vote anymore. I used to think, as I stood in a long voting line, that we have jets that allow me to travel halfway around the nation faster than I can vote for the president. There has to be a better way, but they sure don't want us to find it.

So for me now, it is going to be a waiting game. I am planning on staying here at DIA until roads are clear and transportation gets set up, and then I will make my way to the cabin. I'm very comfortable in my small berth. I am hoping to work with the energy techniques I have used in a clinical setting. I want to somehow develop energy as a placebo or find a way that all people can tap that medical channel so they can use it themselves whenever they need it. I think we all should know more about our own anatomy. The body should not be a mystery. It is the vessel we live in all our lives, and we should know it better than concert violinists know their instruments. I don't know how we have become so distanced from our corporeal selves.

I will volunteer for leadership rotation on the Town Hall if I have to. I will volunteer nonstop on any committee that needs me, and of course I will be available to clean the toilets too. I've learned so much and feel I have grown so much stronger through this journey, but I am anxious to get home. I am sure each of us will go our separate ways from here. Tomorrow morning might be our last small group meditation and I find myself thinking of how much I will miss it.

I am looking forward to tomorrow's meditation but I have

not practiced anything ESP-related by myself so I don't know if I will add anything to the group, but I have done a lot of meditation in the moment and I find myself repeating the "Yod Hey Vah Hey" at down times. When I am feeling stressed, I go straight to my meditation center, do the breathing, hold the grounding with the Earth and try to squeeze in some gratitude exercises. The stress reliever is basically a quick-format version of Isolde's meditation, and it always calms and soothes me and brings me to my center no matter what turmoil is going on around me.

What I have noticed most since I have been participating in all of this mediation stuff is a stilling of my mind. In my old life, it was like there was a little chipmunk sitting on my shoulder chattering away all day about what I had to do, where I was going, what had happened previously. I try not to follow the chipmunk anymore when it tries to take over. I focus on whatever task I am in at present instead of letting my mind wander uselessly. It is comforting to just be in the present and trust that you are exactly where you need to be. I have a new appreciation for the mundane and everyday anyway. I want to be in the present and look around and appreciate what I did not lose.

Tonight I will do my mind link with Mark. I have been trying to do it at the same time each evening. I beam love and pictures of my day to him and the twins. Then I do my gratitude exercises. No matter what, I survived and life is precious. I am so grateful for that. I am grateful the firing of the Mid Regional government went well, and I feel that I actually stepped up for what I believe in for once in my life. I would not have done it without Consuela at my side, but that is what friendship is all about. I am grateful to have good new friends, no matter the circumstance. All this might be unbearable if I were still travelling solo.

Day 9   5:45 a.m.

I slept soundly last night. I think I was at peace and without any doubts about what happened at the summit. I woke up this morning and had a few seconds in which I could not figure out where I was. I have been in so many places and had so many stimuli. A couple of answers flashed through my mind. In the first, I was staying overnight in a youth hostel while traveling. Then I thought no, wait, this is my spaceship compartment. In that hypnopompic way, both felt quite real and logical. I think that just tells me how far reality has stretched at this point. The room is back to feeling like a tiny room on a cruise boat now that I am fully awake.

I am meeting the others in an hour, and then the big contact on the field radio is at 11 a.m.

It feels amazing to think this is almost over. Not over in the real sense, but settled. Like we have crossed some bridges that needed to be crossed and set some precedents. I hope we can get to work and not have to worry if there is going to be a big fight for power and control. To have anyone's son or daughter or spouse or parent to have survived against all odds only to be shot by a fellow countryman over a political idea would madden me.

I am glad the general has decamped to the new continent. To me, it seems as though he is out of the way there and can't do any harm. I guess he won't be doing any harm if the countries that show up share his ideology. Or is it the other way around? Does he want to force everyone's hand on this new continent so he can finally do things his way? Do we even know if he and the rogue militia are still a threat? I wonder also if the Eastern and Western regional governments are going to recognize what we have done here. I know Ian, Isolde, Consuela and Reginald still are planning on going to the East Coast soon. Philip, Jon, Sara and Beatrice want to go to the new continent. Isolde and Ian and their family may need a new place to settle if the chunk of California that housed their hacienda has fallen into the sea, so they might think of settling the new continent as well. I think it is a great idea if regular people go over there and just settle it and start working with whoever else shows up. No weapons allowed. I think a spirit of cooperation would prevail. Especially if lovely people such as Philip and Sara and Isolde and Beatrice began settling there. Let this be our first experiment in non-land ownership. There has never been a time in our recent history that an opportunity like this has presented itself. Usually there has to be messy war and genocide before new land is taken.

I will be happy to stay in my little world in South Park. I will enjoy visiting them when they get themselves all set up and the dust has settled over there. I like to think there is so much land there; it would not be possible to fight over it. I am laughing to myself even as I write that. I guess there will always be the most prized spot, the glorious view or the best land for agriculture.

9:52 a.m.

It has been an exciting morning, and I am walking on air.

The morning held its usual share of surprises. I was the first to arrive at Maria's. Everyone was still getting ready, moving about and in their separate areas and rooms, so I sat on the couch in the living room and watched the kids playing around on the floor. They had these amazing colored, odd-shaped rock crystals that looked far too precious for children to be messing with and somehow reminded me of that wacky panda dream. The kids relaxed after a bit, talking and playing and forgot I was there. I was enjoying listening to their kid conversations. The topic changed at one point, and they began talking about "Atlantis" and the crystals they were going to see when they got there.

Atlantis?

I sat there frozen on the couch for a few moments as it

came together for me. Isolde and her family and who knows who else think the new continent that has risen is the legendary continent of Atlantis, and they think these rock crystals are actually from the old Atlantis. The thought crossed my mind that these people might be a little off, and that I had better get out of there. At that point, Ian walked into the room and his eyes met mine. He picked up the change in my demeanor and his eyes quickly scanned my face. Then I could feel him reach out and tap lightly into my mind -- and he burst into laughter. He called to Consuela and Isolde, who came out of one of the bedrooms. They too did the quick scan, but they did not laugh. They settled on either side of me and cleared the children out of the room. Then they explained everything.

They do believe the continent that has risen is Atlantis. They say they know it because their youngest sister Leah, who is with the parents hunkered down on the East Coast with high-level government officials, has talked about Atlantis since the time she could speak. It was Leah who had gathered the crystals, and one of the reasons the general, our country and other countries might want to be there is a rumored power source on Atlantis that is supposedly more powerful than a thousand nuclear bombs.

The government and general have been involved in exploration for Atlantis for years. They know it was an advanced civilization and the technology had far outpaced our own. What the government is not mentioning is that there are roads and structures still in place on the new continent. Clearly this was a previously inhabited land, inhabited by a people whose highly advanced technology included structures and roads that remain intact after being submerged for thousands of years. Clearly the country that controls the technology on the new continent is going to control the world.

They told me a little about Leah to explain why they had given their youngest sister's belief in Atlantis such credence. In a family of exceptional people, Leah is a standout. From the moment she was born she has been extraordinary. She was doted on by every member of the families, the entire household staff and even the pets. They said you could tell she was special right away because she was checked in like no infant they had ever seen, and then advanced way beyond her age in everything. She trailed her older brothers and sisters whenever she could and absorbed knowledge from them. She could read by the age most toddlers were beginning to talk. By age five she could speak several languages, play a violin well enough to perform with a symphony orchestra and dismantle and then reassemble a car engine if one of her brothers would do the heavy lifting for her. But there was nothing she enjoyed more than being in a group. Whether it was family, social gatherings or school, if it involved group activity she was there. Leah was so advanced, there wasn't a school that could educate her properly, but she really enjoyed going for the group activities. She had graduated from an Ivy League university by the time she was fifteen. She had since spent her time traveling, opting for a world education rather than pursuing formal training in anything.

But from the time she could talk, she has talked about Atlantis, even though she called it something different at first. She talked about Atlantis as if she had just come from there. As she grew, she mentioned it less and less to those outside of the family, but she never wavered in her belief that Atlantis had existed and that it was going to rise again. She couples this with a strong psychic ability. She sounds amazing, especially since she is not yet 18, which is why she is still with her parents.

She could have been just another gifted teenager if she had not started bringing home the crystals. The family took a trip to Mammoth Cave in Kentucky when she was very young and she wandered off one morning and came back in the afternoon with a few small beautiful crystals in strikingly bold colors. They were perfectly shaped and appeared otherworldly, not something a youngster could have made or had enough money to buy. There were subsequent trips to different locations all over the world, during which she would go and get crystals. They were the only decorative things she would keep in her room. She taught Ian and Isolde and Consuela about them and how to use them.

She has a side to her nature which her family refers to as fey. She is at home in the world and much attuned to nature. When she was very young she would disappear for hours at a time, frightening the entire household and triggering a manhunt. As she got older and her family became more accustomed to her disappearances, she would leave for days at a time. When the family traveled to foreign countries, she loved nothing more than to disappear and immerse herself in the culture. She would try and learn about the people and try to pick up as much of the language and local lore as she could in a short time. Isolde says she is so beautiful that you almost cannot look at anything else when she is in a room, and the family always had to trust that she would come to no harm -- and she never has.

(I think I wrote that Isolde is by far the most beautiful person I have ever seen, so I can't even imagine what her sister must look like.)

After the family took an extended trip to Egypt, the crystals Leah brought home became more amazing, and they wanted to show me one as proof. Isolde went to her backpack to pull out the crystal Leah had given her long ago. It was the shape and size of a piece of loose-leaf paper and beautiful in clarity and form. Isolde handed it to me and told me to look in it, calmly focus and to think of Mark. As I focused, I could feel the energy centering in the tablet, and a live picture of Mark and the babies formed, then got fuzzy and disappeared as I got excited. I closed my eyes, held the crystal and the thought of him and the kids, and calmed my mind for a few moments as I chanted "Yod Hey Vah Hey." When I opened my eyes and looked into the tablet, a clear picture of the three of them formed. They were in the front room of the cabin, and the room looked to be fine. Mark was getting three towels out of a chest and it looked like maybe they were about to bathe. Even as the question formed in my mind, I could see a still shot in Mark's mind of where he was going. It seemed that a natural hot spring had formed on our land and they were headed there to soak. His beard was growing out but otherwise they all looked just the same as the day I had kissed them goodbye. I was so happy to see them that I started crying, and in my mind I was saying "Mark" over and over and over. Then I saw him look up and look around as if he had heard it. He shook his head as if to clear it, but he smiled his little half smile. That smile told me he knew I was alive and kicking. He could feel me thinking of him, I just knew it. I started crying harder, and the screen went completely blank as I lost my focus.

Consuela took the tablet from my hands, giving me a look of sympathy. She said I could practice with the crystal tablet later to become better at tuning in and even trying to make contact. She said crystals actually were used as communication devices back in the old Atlantis. Crystals require knowledge and some tuning to use them effectively, and the people on Atlantis were adept at it.

Isolde explained that I must have lived in Atlantis in a couple of past lives, because that is the only way I would have been able to tune into the tablet and see what I wanted to see right away. Some people can peer in and see only a perfect crystal.

After they told the story of Leah and showed me the crystal tablet, they asked me to come to the East Coast with them early tomorrow to meet Leah. My immediate thought was, "No way. I am staying right here at DIA until those roads are clear." They explained that they thought it was going to be hard for people to do this firing-the-government thing without some organization. Without regular people stepping up to do their part, we might be in danger of going through another cycle of war at this juncture in history. If regular people step up at this point, however, we may be able to use this new energy to make things happen in a way that paves the way for a peaceful outcome. The way to do this is going to be doing what we have been doing since the beginning, they said: Be the town crier, going about and letting people know there are peaceful options and then stepping up to help with organizing and just talking to people and sharing and helping link people to one another.

Our mission is not over here just because we have made

some inroads at the Mid Regional, they said. It is not like the end of a movie where there is denouement and everyone lives happily ever after. The other two governments might just take a vote today to act as majority, do whatever they choose and call it democracy. So Ian wants one of the first orders of the day to be setting up a rotation of flights to start getting people over to the East Coast and West Coast. He wants to get as many people to both coasts as soon as possible because dissemination of information will be so important.

I wondered if they were going to tell everyone they thought Atlantis had risen. They said they were not going to make some general announcement because most people's reaction would probably be much like my own, but it is not like they feel it is a secret. They will talk about it to anyone who is interested or wants to listen, but they will not break out the crystals for just anyone. Leah is really the Atlantis expert, and they are sure she is talking away to anyone who will listen back East -- if she still is in a bunker and not already on the new continent. There is no holding Leah back.

Ian, Isolde and Consuela want to talk the others from our original group into joining them in going to the East Coast as well. I did not think the idea would be a hard sell for the others, I just did not know if I wanted to go over and continue. Then I just knew I would have to go. For all the same reasons I left Civic Center in the first place, to prove the civic responsibility. I must step up and stand behind my beliefs in what is right and what is needed. I think this is one of those times in life that circumstance is greater than the individual. In times such as these I believe ordinary people have to stand up for what they believe is right. I cannot keep wanting others to make the stand and then hope for the outcome that I want. I am a little frightened to push for my agenda because what if it is selfish and not right for everyone? I guess I have to follow my intuition about everything now. It has gotten me this far.

When the others arrived at the apartment, Isolde explained everything briefly and then said she hoped they would continue on to the East Coast. They all agreed immediately, which solidified my decision.

We did the small group meditation, which included Consuela. We took it up yet another notch when we went out to the hangar -- and levitated the cargo plane.

I can't believe I can blithely write things like that now. It was as if all of us were even more focused in our new mission and our group energy had a new confidence. I don't know about all of this past-life stuff, whether I was ever on Atlantis as an adept and that is how I am able to help accomplish these things but I do think the entire group was feeling more lighthearted, even in the face of governmental upheaval, so we decided to try something big.

Ian led us out to the hangar and showed us a light green crystal he wanted us to focus on to help magnify the level of group energy. He then led us in the levitation exercise that lifted the cargo plane.

I was exhilarated by this exercise, but afterward wondered why we were manipulating the plane. Ian gave several reasons. The practical applications might include mind linking together quickly and confidently to get the plane over or through a rough spot safely if we were to lose an engine or three on our way to the East Coast. He said it was also for peaceful resistance. We could use the thought-forward trick to form an image that makes us look like a stand of trees rather than a group of people. Or, if we had to, we could maybe stop a falling missile with a group link and divert it back over the ocean. If we grew really strong, he said, maybe we could stop a fighter jet in midflight, or thought-project a vision of a large wall or a river that would be hard to cross. If push comes to shove, he said, we want to have some tools in our belt that don't involve shooting one another.

Ian said it is important that groups work together to build an individual's confidence in the ability to do amazing things such as levitating a cargo plane. Then that individual can take that confidence out and show others that amazing things can be done. It will give everyone the confidence to try to work with the new energy and the confidence that they can do this. When they do, he said, they will show other people who will show others in turn -- and soon we'll be looking at large groups of people out there who feel confident manipulating this new energy. The faster we wake up to the reality that this energy can be manipulated, he said, the faster we can move humanity forward to innovation we cannot even fathom. He thinks the idea for getting that moving faster is for people such as him and Isolde, who feel comfortable doing so, to show other individuals how and what can be done. People such as myself who are shown things like telekinesis learn that it can be done and then turn around, practice and learn how to do it and show others. In this way a huge network is built of people showing one another. Energy has become easy to use, he said, and it is part of our soul mission here on Earth to learn, teach and evolve. We are all connected to the energy flow around us, and every single object vibrates with energy. From there, you move into the laws of how the universe works. Ian laughingly said he is still trying to figure that out, but that he would keep me posted.

After levitating the plane we went out into the common areas. We do make an interesting group, and I understand how we influence people through our actions and not our words. I think there is also something about being attractive, intelligent and fit that helps us get the message across.

I know Ian is right that we create something here together as a group that we could not create as individuals, and I am beginning to think that I am a part of it because I must have a soul mission. Our little group is getting our special energy revved up for something, and I don't know what it is or if Ian knows what it is. I have to see this as a mission, acknowledge that there is no going back, that everything is going to play out and I seem to have a role in it. Once you have seen a plane rise in the air and know you are helping to do that with your mind because you can feel the almost physical hum that is being generated, it is hard to think three-dimensionally anymore.

In the common areas people were quiet again and

reflective, but at least there were a lot of them out and about. Again I got the feeling that people were looking around for organization, for what they needed to be doing, so naturally Isolde began to put out the word for everyone to meet forty-five minutes before eleven so we can do a large group meditation. The rest of us followed her lead and began walking around telling everyone about the meditation and to spread the word.

We checked in with the field monitors and learned there had not been much activity on the radio between the Eastern and Western regional governments. It seems everyone is keeping a low profile and wondering what everyone else is going to do. I wondered if the radio communication was really the only communication going on between leaders, and whether the general knows about what is happening here in the Mid Region and about the crystals on Atlantis.

Ian and Isolde want to leave early tomorrow morning in the cargo plane, fly to Brush to get the dogs, and then fly to whatever airport is nearest the underground facility their parents and Leah are at. They are hoping after the communication on the radio today that word of what happened here will get out to the general populace and nudge all the leaders out into the open to begin talking and interacting with the people. The leaders must have begun to come to the same conclusion that people will want to be involved in decision making, but the highest-ranking members of the government are on the East Coast and it is they who have the final say. For all we know, the government might feel free to halt air travel or put us under house arrest for inciting rebellion.

I wonder what the big vote at 11 a.m. is really going to be about, or if it will be a vote at all, after what has happened at the Mid Regional. I have a feeling we will be addressed on the field radio, so I am off to the auditorium. I wanted to take some time to write down all my thoughts before other events crowd in and I forget how things went down.

Overlying everything is seeing Mark and the babies on that crystal tablet. I know I will be back to them soon and that this is going to come to a good resolution. In times of crisis it takes nice normal people to stand up for what they feel is right.

I am confident that Mark knows I am alive and making my way back to him. I am sure we will laugh at the circuitous route I took, but I am also sure I am on the right track here and that he would be doing the same thing.

4:36 p.m.

It was the president who spoke on the field radio. He is the final decision maker and has the power to call out the military, so it makes sense.

It was not interactive at all, and there was no vote. He made a moving speech that made it seem they were really going to take this cooperation instead of leadership under consideration, and the speech sounded as if it was being given from far, far underground. He went on to say everyone is safe and there are plans in place for how to proceed, and we Americans all want the same results. No one is going to move against anyone else's wishes or raise a weapon, he said. The focus is on clearing and rebuilding everywhere. As soon as things really settle, he said, the leaders will emerge and there will be decision making that involves everyone.

It felt like they think we are an isolated pocket that has to be mollified and placated for now, and they know they have more strength over there and are going to move forward with whatever is planned. I see even more clearly now why it is so important for people to go to the two coasts and the new continent. If people don't make a stand here, our wishes will be steamrolled and it will be business as usual. I am beginning to realize the world will be focused on this new continent. For all we know, we already have a military presence on Atlantis. I wondered why Leah wasn't doing more to organize the people on the East Coast. When I asked Ian about it, he laughed and said she is not like that.

Since we were gathered for the announcement and feeling

at peace from the meditation, the people of DIA decided by vote after the speech to move ahead with our own agenda and finish getting things set up as we thought they should be. We have formed interim committees that will be in place for three months, after which we'll reassess; the members were selected by lottery. The flights start tomorrow. Neighborhoods are going to be cleared from the airport toward downtown to make buildings habitable for those who do not want to stay at the airport. All sorts of other things were decided. It felt very productive. We addressed not only the concerns of the people of the United States but also those from other countries. So many people had valuable input. Even children got elected to the committees. If you are fourteen or up, you get a say and can be a part of the process. Civic responsibility is going to have to be a key to the new setup since we elected not to keep the government.

I do think politicians here in the Mid Region have realized nothing is going to be the same in this new environment, but I am sure many of them don't see this as a big power struggle. They see our group as a moth flying toward the flame, whereas I think we see it as an interim leadership cooperative that could work until we get everything cleared and rebuilt.

Our group spent the rest of the day mobilizing to get people over to the East and West coasts. We don't feel the staff here likes the fact that anyone is flying around on their own, but they are not going to try to control airspace right now. I don't think they would actively lend us any fuel, either. We are not the only ones who are planning on flying ourselves over to a coast. We are getting word that here and there planes are being taken from the small airports surrounding DIA, and the number of people signing up for flights from here is overwhelming. I believe people are thinking they had better make a move before the military tries to shut down the airspace, but things could disintegrate quickly if people start grabbing planes and everyone does anything they want here. Maybe that is what the government is hoping for.

There are pilots here at DIA who have volunteered to

begin ferrying people over to major airports on both coasts. We have announced our intentions on the radio, and as usual, we did not hear a yay or a nay from elected leadership.

I am growing more curious about what is really going on, and I know we have to make our move before we get brushed off like a mosquito by a government that is working its own agenda. I think this Mid Regional situation has taken leaders by surprise, and they want to proceed with caution, yet cannot effectively communicate with one another about how to go about things. I wonder if the people on the other two coasts are receiving mixed messages -- or any messages at all. We will see if they are contending with more of a military presence across the river on the East Coast. We know the general was headquartered over there in a geographical safe zone, and that he and his group probably came out pretty early after the catastrophe to make a big grab for weapons and supplies, leaving the citizenry feeling vulnerable.

I am off to the south mess hall to meet Reginald and Bea. They have been talking with some different military outfits, and it will be interesting to hear what they learned. I also want to discuss the proposal Ian and Isolde put before us this morning as we were leaving the hangar. They want to demonstrate the levitation of the cargo plane to some science and engineer types who have shown interest. The scientists have some energy-measuring equipment they would like to use while we lift the aircraft. I understand we have to do this to give it credence, but I am nervous I won't be able to hold the focus under pressure and will throw off the group if others are measuring and onlookers are watching skeptically. I know we have to show others, just as Ian and Isolde showed us, I just don't know if I am ready and should be included. I think Ian, Isolde and Consuela could do this, just the three of them, but I do understand there also have to be regular people represented who step up and show that they have been able to manipulate the energy, that this will be the "new normal" and can be a routine part of life, not something that needs to be feared. If we show skeptics or people of a scientific bent and they accept it right away and get excited about it, I think that would trickle down. The more common it is, the less likely people are to label it magic or witchcraft or whatever else people tend to call something they cannot see with their eyes. I understand how seeing rational, normal people stepping up and doing this encourages others. I myself believed in nothing but science, and now I have quickly come around to extra sensory perception and am thinking of showing others I can help levitate a large plane, all in a span of a week. If all goes well with the observers tonight, I can see them believing in it and practicing it together so they can then begin showing others what can be done. And the lore spreads from here.

A part of what helped me use ESP for the first time when I created the image of a wall from a table was having seen Isolde and Ian raise that red ball and then letting the belief that it can be done sink in. People should know not to be afraid of this ability or the fact that we all have it and can now develop it rather than repress and convolute it. What surprises me is that I am enjoying stepping up and working with this ability, which is so outside what I would have ever thought I could be comfortable with. That I would actually look forward to participating in group meditations is a huge leap, so joining energy with a small group to physically manipulate energy borders on staggering for me. It is important to show how, as a group of strangers, we were able to bond together in a short time and can now manipulate energy to such a degree that we can lift a plane into the air. Because these people are also living closely and having these shared experiences, they are noticing the new energy and should know they can develop this stuff as a group as we have and as the military has. Some will look for guidance.

The key to feeling comfortable in developing all of this is the meditation and focusing within. Meditate throughout the day for five seconds here or two minutes there instead of letting the mind chatter take over. The chant "Yod Hey Vah Hey," in combination with the intake and outtake of breathing and the focus on being in the moment are tools that a novice like me or anyone else can use to help calm and center, no matter the circumstance. I think the military sees it as a tool, like a headset for communication, and have been using it casually in that way. Military people generally are focused individuals, so it is a tool they could easily further develop. The general and his group are probably utilizing it as well for who knows what purpose.

I am going to pack up my backpack yet again, since we leave so early tomorrow morning. I am a pro at this now, compared with that first packing under the table. I can almost laugh at what happened to that old backpack now, except that it held so many dear memories and I did not want to say goodbye to it.

After dinner, we will meet in the big auditorium to devise further lottery systems, our process for deciding everything from who is going to the East and West coasts and the new continent to who will be interim leaders here at DIA and who will be in charge of what. Committees of specialists for things such as electrical wiring or pipe repair have to be volunteered for. It is a fascinating system that might work, and at least is fair for now. Some masters of organization have really stepped up here and I feel there are many who are devoted to the cause and will continue to devote their time to making sure this cooperation goes smoothly. I will see this through to the end, even though it feels as though I am zigzagging back and forth when I should be helping clear the roads up to the mountain passes to get to my family.

10:36 p.m.

We demonstrated the levitation of the cargo plane for seventeen people. The scene was pretty amazing as the wide plane rose steadily into the air. As they saw the plane rise, the onlookers' excitement built and a wonderful thing happened. Their energy caught fire and joined our small group's energy and made the levitation that much easier. Afterward, they asked a lot of questions about how we do it and showed us how their energy-reading meters had topped out.

It was harder to explain or show another individual how the mind link and manipulation of energy works than I thought it would be. Our group of seven that came together at Civic all seemed be able to link in with one another quickly. It makes me think maybe we have known one another in past lives and have worked together like this before, and that maybe we are drawn to one another for those very reasons.

No longer does ESP have to be an unknown, scary thing on the fringes of society. It will have to be acknowledged as just another form of energy we need to learn how to plug into.

The military people Reginald and Bea spoke to seemed relieved that leadership has not issued the general call yet. They want organization as quickly as we do, but after you have been through something like this your perspective changes. You don't want to harm one another. You can't believe you made it through alive, and you want to do something with the gift you have been given instead of fighting with one another or wanting to acquire things again or think about defending our shores. To the last man and woman, I know the military will always stand up for what is right, and they all said they still are ready and willing when the call does come.

While we feel there will probably need to be some sort of government in the near future, we all agreed that we will continue to take these interim town hall votes at very regular periods. What a great problem to have when there are too many people again. Violence is not happening as it used to. I think it all hearkens back to having survived the catastrophe. Everything and every person feel precious, and everyone is cooperating to the best of his or her ability and is truly considered equal. The playing field is now very level. The only thing people have to give is time and effort. Add that to the fact that we have plenty of supplies on hand and no shortages that we know of in the near future.

Perhaps the goal of humanity at this juncture is the evolution to a higher understanding of love, peace and harmony, as the songs say. There will always be times in history when people have to stand for peace even in the face of great discomfort and fear. If we acknowledge that physical reality is not the only reality, that we are all one and that it is our mission to wake up to that truth, then maybe -- just maybe -- we can really make a leap into peace here and begin working on interesting things besides war against one another.

I must call it a night. The excitement has been unreal, as usual. That sentence should cancel itself out or something, I have written it so often. I look forward to lying in my bunk and thinking of Mark and the kids and doing my grateful exercise and meditation. We will do a group meditation at the plane tomorrow before the short flight back to Brush and then the longer flight across that raging river.

Day 10 4:35 a.m.

I slept soundly again, with no odd dreams that I remember. Feeling safe in my surroundings led to deep, restful sleep. I am feeling really healthy. In fact, I have never felt better. I have always been very serious about health and fitness so I am in excellent shape, but I still feel as if my body is still generating that extra adrenaline that takes it up a notch. I don't need as much sleep. All of this might be because I am still in fight-or-flight mode. Or it could be the new heightened energy.

I am enjoying a cup of hot coffee. This might be my last for a while, since I am leaving most of my things here in a storage locker, including my small propane stove to heat water. We had to pack really light since we are adding Consuela and then picking up the extra weight of the dogs, and we have heard that the winds over the river can be tricky so we want to be light with plenty of fuel.

We plan to land in West Virginia. I have a feeling Ian and Isolde have known all along where their parents and Leah are. It feels as if they are orchestrating this a bit, but I have given up asking myself why. I think having lived such a wealthy life exposed them to so much in their schooling and travel that this seems the ultimate adventure. Or is it that they really believe all this soul evolution and reincarnation stuff and feel this is a soul mission. The two of them and Consuela and their extended family are some of the nicest, most genuine people I have ever met, so I have to think they really believe they are here for this very specific purpose. If they can help us all through, orchestrate away. I have tied my fate to theirs and feel I have known all of them before. The way we had the instant connections and the way we are all able to mind link is pretty amazing.

Hopefully, this is the last leg for me. I feel we have gotten a lot done here at DIA. I think we are full steam ahead on organization for all basic functions, extending outward from the airport and linking up and rebuilding with individuals and encampments. Fuel supplies are going to be the premium. We have our stash at Brush, so we don't need to worry, but soon the leadership is going to have to release the supplies to the committees to debate where we stand and how we want it dispersed.

We will be staying in West Virginia at least a day and playing it by ear from there. We might fly in to a situation where the people are very comfortable and don't want things to change. If things are being run the way they want and they are happy then we don't have much to do. We just want to make sure word spreads on the ground about what happened with the Mid Regional government summit and the fact that the new continent might have an immense power source that our own general and other countries might be running toward. We might spend a couple of days, demonstrate the town hall format and some of the meditation exercises, and maybe the levitation. Mainly, we have to get to the seat of power, and then we can better assess what is happening.

I hope to write when I am settled over the water. Our stop in Brush will be brief. It should take right around four hours to get to West Virginia. Other convoys also are going over today and fanning out to the surrounding airports. It makes me feel better that we won't be the only ones in the airspace.

4:25 p.m.

We made it to West Virginia. No one was exaggerating when they said the winds over the river are tricky. They buffet you back and forth and pull strongly in one direction suddenly. It is hard to believe the continent is the same continent. There is so much water now, and so much destruction and rubble. It is still raining lightly, so it is not as if you can see the minute detail of it all. The heaps of rubble of what used to be a town or city are fairly evident. There were people out and about, and as we flew over they would wave at us, excited to finally see regular planes in the air again, I think. There seem to be more people camped out near roads, the roads are beginning to be clear and there is a lot more movement than we saw when we originally left Denver. It was heartening to see.

We got together early this morning for the meditation, which was surprisingly short. I know Ian and Isolde were eager to get going. We made it to Brush in no time and saw people getting ready for flights out. There were crews out working in the fields and roads were being cleared by heavy machinery. I know there are plans in place to continue working on infrastructure such as systems for running water and getting bridges back in place so people can move to and fro. Engineers are coming up with plans to get water from the creeks and rivers and purify it more efficiently here at Brush.

No one but Ian and Isolde got off the plane in Brush. It was somewhat nostalgic to fly along the outskirts of the town and into the airport. Ian landed the plane next to one of the back hangars where he had stored a bunch of extra fuel. He had gathered plenty and put it aside before the military showed up and started pumping their planes full. Then he whistled the whistle and about three minutes later the pack of dogs came with Rue in the lead and seeming somewhat eager, at least for Rue. Jon had sectioned off the back of the plane for them and secured it with a cage-like enclosure in case we ran into turbulence. The dogs went in there and settled down. I could tell Rue was not happy to be on the plane, but the other dogs seemed glad to be with us again.

The flight went well until we got to the outer banks of the Mississippi split. We were still flying low to the ground with no instruments, and the flight was fairly calm. Then the pockets of turbulence began to build and the plane started buckling. I am not a good flyer and instinctively wanted to withdraw inside to do my centering meditation but Isolde called on us to focus as a group and to work on stabilizing the plane as we moved through the air. As we all centered ourselves on the plane, it did level out and there was not as much buckling.

The split is gradual at first, tapering into a canyon with a truly raging river at the bottom. White and frothing in the middle, it was washing up against the outer walls in waves on either side. There was a lot of what looked like big debris churning through the water. I am sure the river grabbed and is continuing to grab anything in its path.

I felt we were flying a little close for comfort. It always helps to look at Isolde and Bea in these situations. They radiate calm and intensity. When Bea feels the attention, she will always look over at you and give you one of those cheerleading-type smiles that make you smile back, even if it feels fake.

I was not the only one uneasy. Reginald seems to mirror my emotions and thoughts in every way, and the dogs were also restless as we crossed the water. Of course it was Reginald and I who had to continue looking out the only two windows in the plane. I was glad to finally make it across.

Across the river, the landscape was about the same: major devastation everywhere the eye could see. The smaller towns with smaller buildings tended to look better. There was the occasional strip or house or building that had survived unscathed. People were moving about in the smaller towns, repairing buildings and clearing the roads from what we could see. After we got across the river a ways, I moved away from the window.

Near the end of our flight, we were joined by a fighter jet and escorted to the Greenbrier airport. I wondered how the military knew where we would be, since there had been no radio communication during our flight and radar does not exist. I could feel our group's minds reaching out to explore that of the fighter pilot, and suddenly in all of our minds there was Leah. I could feel her mind link with Ian, Isolde and Consuela, and I knew everyone else could feel her as well because we all stirred when we felt her link with them and reach for us. I thought at first she was in the fighter jet with the pilot. Then I realized she was the pilot of the fighter jet.

She led us to a good-sized airport that had been fully cleared and looked normal. It was a beautiful reunion scene between her, Ian, Isolde and Consuela, and then between Leah and Rue the wolf dog. Leah is amazing to look at, and I will say she has officially taken over as the most beautiful person I have ever seen. Her beauty is striking and more defined than Isolde's, as though Isolde was the mold and Leah is the final product. The word "ethereal" comes to mind when I think of her. She seems to emanate light from within. She is as tall as Ian and as she unfolded herself from the cockpit I wondered about height requirements for those jets. After she greeted her family, she walked over and embraced each of us in turn. She did not say much. She communicated with her eyes and body language, and her thoughts were right there in your mind.

Then there was the reunion of Leah and Rue. Rue was standing, not pacing, closer to the group than he normally will stand to people and looking steadily at Leah. When she had finally greeted everyone she turned to Rue. They walked toward one another, and Rue was looking at Leah instead of through her. When their eyes met, I could tell communication was happening. As I stood next to Isolde, she explained that it was Leah who had found Rue and nursed him back to health in the wild and Leah who had raised and trained the wolfhounds. As the catastrophe loomed and the family headed out in different directions she assigned the wolfhounds to Isolde and Rue to Ian to see them through. All animals gravitate to her and she responds in kind, Isolde said, and it was amazing to see and feel it in action.

Leah has an uncanny ability to look at you, somehow center in on the core of your being and read you like an open book. I felt as if I had given up every secret to her the moment I looked at her, and that she loved me all the more for any flaws she may have seen. She is not yet twenty-one but feels older than everyone, including Jon.

This airport has a good military presence. Military is everywhere you look. You can tell who is military because they wear camouflage. The setup at this airport is much like the other temporary camps we have seen since the disaster.

Leah led us all into a meeting-type room and asked Ian and Isolde for a full report, and filled them in on the whereabouts of the general and the parents. The parents are still underground in a reinforced city much like the one at DIA. They are content and will not be emerging for a while. Leah has been exploring and flying since they opened the door to the bunker and deemed it somewhat safe to be outside.

She has been to Atlantis several times and has seen where the general is camped. His is not the first or only presence on the new continent. He had massed his forces near here, up the road at a state forest, but never seemed to have any intention of trying to take over the leadership here, gain control of the people or kidnap anyone in power. His goal seems to have been grabbing weapons and supplies, and then running for the new continent. Leah seemed thrilled that the general and his force were there.

She let us know that our Mid Regional summit had made not a ripple on this side of the country. It had been presented to the rest of the world like some sort of Wild West stand by a very small minority of people.

The unconfirmed rumor here is that a big military mobilization will be heading to the new continent soon. There will be more organization once they get there.

The military have been a strong presence here since people began emerging to help organize and clean up. The order of things went up right away, so there has not been the bonding together and interdependence of the regular people that we had in Denver. People just did whatever the military, which was in direct contact with the highest leadership in the land, said to do. There has been much clearing and rebuilding here, but no group sing-along or group meditation or anything that might bring them together.

Everyone has kept somewhat to themselves, and our little group aims to change that by creating a spark. Leah wants us to spread out and let everyone know that a group that has come over from the middle of the continent has news of big happenings and some interesting objects for a show and tell.

The military is controlling the airspace and everything else over here. No one person is challenging anything because they know the orders are being given by the commander in chief and they had the recent scare from the general, so we also want to let people know there is another option in the mix. We plan to go around today and begin issuing our invitation for people to gather tomorrow to hear what we have to say.

I was curious to know why Leah had not put together these group meditations or tried to do some organization over here, especially since she and her parents were hunkered down with some high-level members of the government, but I am finding Leah does not say much in general and seems only vaguely checked in to the process. Clearly, she has her own agenda. She is incredible, but her presence is somewhat disinterested, as though she would just as soon disappear into the woods for a few days as remember that there might be something important planned.

Leah said she will be telling the story of past-life Atlantis tomorrow to recruit people to go over there for the mission of rebuilding that continent to its full glory. She says she has some items from Atlantis she will use for a show and tell to convince any non-believers.

She suggested to Reginald that he might talk to the military leadership here so that no one gets the wrong perception about what we did in Denver. It is important that everyone put all information out in the open so that no fear or suspicion is created. It turns out that Reginald holds a fairly high rank in the military.

I think their family mission is going to be the gentle introduction of this new continent as the new/old Atlantis and recruiting people to settle it peacefully. Apparently, Leah will spend today doing who knows what, and tomorrow wishes to lead a large group meditation which will be followed by the show and tell presentation aiming to prove that the new continent is Atlantis risen, followed by a question-and-answer session.

She said she then plans to head over to Atlantis and does not plan to return, and said she hopes to see us all there. She gets so excited when she talks about returning to Atlantis for good that we can feel her energy thrumming. Leah is Bea's new Isolde, and I can see she plans on being wherever Leah is. Clearly Ian, Isolde, Consuela and the rest of the gang will also be going to the new continent, so by default it looks as though I am headed to Atlantis tomorrow.

Leah gave us a quick tour of the airport and showed us to a large room where we are able to unroll our bedrolls and have relative privacy for the night. They have a form of running water here, but it is a more rudimentary setup than DIA's for sure. There are the usual mix of travelers and locals, and way more multinational cultures than were back at our Brush airport. However, this place feels like more of a way station than a permanent stop. Our convoys from Denver are likely to be the talk of the town, we hope, and also will bring more groups that can go talk to people and take advantage of any interest in Leah's meditation tomorrow.

I have tasked myself with going to the clinic they have set up here to talk with the medical personnel and encourage them to attend Leah's meditation tomorrow. Reginald will speak with the high-level military. Jon and Philip will head for churches and schools to spread the word. Isolde, Ian and Consuela are going to visit with the parents and Bea plans to try to follow Leah around today. All of us are telling anyone who will listen about the event tomorrow.

I look forward to going to the hospital here. A small facility is up and running. The streets are so clear here that I want to take a walk over there. I am curious to see what their medical efforts look like, how they are staffing and if they have noticed a new energy in themselves and in their patients. It will be good to talk some shop and maybe even put some of my own theories forward and see if they are willing to experiment a little with group energy.

This will be one of my first forays alone since crawling out through the dog door in Denver, and I must admit I am a little nervous and shy. I have always felt more comfortable in a group or as an observer, which is why I gave myself this mission. I need to learn to step up on a more individual basis to show what I know. I need to perhaps introduce my speed-healing theory and how I think it works, and let my colleagues know this new energy might be something medical professionals can work with. I reassure myself that I am going to a setting where I feel comfortable and confident with my peers and that they need to be encouraged to attend Leah's meditation.

This is a perfect dry run for me, I suppose, if I am to bring this energy to the fore in my everyday life and teach it to others. I know I can generate healing energy after what I did on the road with Neil, the drunken guy with the infected tooth. Then when my illusion of the wall actually worked, and when we as a group levitated that plane and drew the spectators' energy, it gave me the confidence of knowing these abilities are here to stay, are strengthened by groups and will only get stronger as we talk about it and work with it. I need to be able to communicate that to my peers.

I keep thinking of that crystal tablet and being able to use it again. It felt so organic in my hands, like a natural extension of myself. I love holding the picture of Mark and the kids going out to that hot spring in my mind, and I can't wait to see it. I think if he had one of those crystal tablets we could have easily communicated. It seemed to me like a high-powered laptop, and I am sure it was used in that way. It makes me think about crystal technology in old transistor radios, or in televisions that used liquid crystal display technology to create a clear picture. I think the way it works is that the crystal acts as a semiconductor and magnifier.

I wonder if there could be crystals that facilitate healing. It would make sense to magnify the energy I feel I can tap into, focus it on the crystal to magnify it and then link to the patient's energy, as Ian had us do with the light green crystal before we levitated the plane. Add that to the energy of the helpers on the other side. The crystal in the middle could tie all the healing energy together, magnify it, or act as a placebo.

I am writing just to procrastinate at this point. I need to get out there.

It is funny to think I intend to go to a medical clinic where I will tell a strange group of my peers about a super-speed healing experience I had, and then let them know I can also help levitate a plane, that I think the new continent that has risen is Atlantis, and then ask them to join me tomorrow in a large group meditation where we will hear details of a culture many thought mythical. Everything in that scenario really would have surprised the person I was a month ago, and I cannot help but wonder what my colleagues will think.

I wonder what I would have thought if Isolde would have told me in one of those first couple of days we spent together at Civic Center that she and her family have had ESP for a long time and that the continent of Atlantis had risen and they planned on going there and I probably would be going with her. I would have run the other way, of course, thinking she was beautiful and mentally unbalanced.

11:36 p.m.

It was a great experience at the medical clinic. I went over and spent several hours in conversation and enjoyed a meal with colleagues there. An amazing group has gathered. They have noticed the new energy and experimented with it as well.

What I noticed initially as I walked through town was that the rubble had been cleared but there were not a lot of people out. A sort of divisiveness hung in the air, and I thought I had figured out what had caused it. It was because government and the military took over the clearing and rebuilding right away, and people seem to have fallen in and let everything be organized for them. After cleaning up in the general vicinity there has been no direction, and people gravitated where they would. There did not seem to have been exploration of new things outside the boundaries of what was done in the past because everything was status quo, organized and comfortable already.

There is not group energy here to speak of. The doctors gravitated to the hospital, the city planners and some architects drifted together, and some of the other professions created guilds of sorts, but mostly everyone has been working on their individual residence or pet projects.

I feel that the difference in the development of energy lies in working together. When I was on the tour at DIA, we came across a dentist who was gathering eggs in a free-range coop in the live-animal holding area. I knew he had been a dentist because he was surrounded by five children who were enraptured by a story he was telling about drilling his first cavity in dental school. He was using a chicken to demonstrate the patient, and it was a hilarious tale. I felt the dentist was getting the chance to do what he wanted to do that day: working with the livestock but at the same time he was passing knowledge and a love of his profession to the children. People at DIA were following their everyday professions while also fostering a spirit of cooperation because the military had not stepped in to do everything. I am sure the dentist was practicing dentistry there in some form, but I felt he was also following a curiosity or passion or whatever by working with the animals and the children. An amazing crossover was happening there. It does not feel as though they have developed that here. Or maybe they have done it underground and I am not feeling it.

It was most interesting to see what the doctors have come up with here. And it was all doctors again; no nurses at the clinic. They have indeed detected the new energy and began using it; they call what they are doing biofeedback research. They have come to pretty much the same conclusion as I that the patient has to be taught that our cells have consciousness and our thoughts and spoken words affect them, so we need to consciously use thought and verbal biofeedback on our physical selves, encouraging the cells to repair themselves instead of using medicine as the intermediary.

When we are hurt or become ill, we tend to become fearful. In the past, medical personnel would use verbiage such as, "We are going to fight this" or "We can beat this." There should never be a war against your own body. Instead of fighting and fearing that part of the body that is experiencing a disease, a patient can be instructed by the doctor to send waves of love and healing energy and mentally visit the afflicted areas as he or she would a sick friend in the hospital, talking to the afflicted area and wishing it a speedy recovery, just as one would to the sick friend. The patient then visualizes a perfect outcome, the area fully healed and the whole body thriving with health. That is the number one thing they do, and it sounds like a type of interactive positive visualization.

Secondly, the patient is encouraged to speak out loud to the body to tell it what has to be done and ask the body to partner in this healing process. Instructions are given out loud to the body on how to heal. It is important to vocalize and validate the illness to bring it into the open to be addressed instead of being hidden away and left to fester, fostering fear of the illness. The patient can go deeper if he or she feels comfortable doing so, having a conversation with the illness in which the malady is asked whether it has a message or anything to say to the body.

Then there is the laying of the patient's own hands on the body -- on the affected area, if possible -- and picturing this light, healing wind or energy flowing through every cell. That is the third part of the biofeedback. It's what they call the dance of light, where pure love and light pours into every cell of the being and vibrates with the joy of being alive as the patient lays hands over the afflicted area.

I really liked what they are doing here, how interactive it is and how it involves patients in their own recovery instead of prescribing medication to treat symptoms. The doctors said it had been going well with the people they had been treating. They were hoping to put it to good use for the longer-term patients and see great results. Someone had also come up with the idea of giving anatomy instruction along with any diagnosis and recovery option, so patients know what they are working with. Along with fearing the unknown, people tend to fear their own body because they don't understand how it works. If doctors teach patients about how it works, it can seem much more like a machine that breaks down and can easily be fixed. I felt this was my same idea of giving anatomy instruction to people, and I was glad to see other doctors thinking the same way. A creative idea will sometimes bloom in a couple of different places at once.

We talked about how our culture has devolved into a society in which we want a pill to fix any ailment when there is much more that goes into any illness. And they aren't going to get around to making more pills for a long time.

I am curious to see how many people show up for the group meditation tomorrow. I presented it more as an informational session about what is happening in other parts of the country and talked a little about the new continent being in the same geographical location that Atlantis was rumored to have been. Then I told them about the crystal tablet I had handled and the people I had met and how we had developed strong ties and are working together with the new energy. I could not bring myself to mention that we had levitated a cargo plane together. Even so, my colleagues were far more receptive than I thought they would be, which led me to tell them about my experience out on the road with Neil of the infected tooth when I had facilitated speed-healing and felt I had tapped into a sort of medical channel that actively involved discarnate souls helping us from the other side. They were surprisingly receptive to that as well. They were also open to my idea that doctors should be mediators or channelers of this healing energy, connecting the patient with their higher energy and a higher energy on the other side. We agreed that biofeedback was taking advantage of those same channels. Like medicine men or shaman or anything of the sort, the doctor should almost act as the placebo for the healing in addition to giving whatever physical assistance or medicine or whatever knowledge they can bring to the situation. On the flip side, doctors will have to be more involved with the patient. It's like my grandfather, the old country doctor, who knew his patients and knew a bit about what was going on in their lives. He dispensed as much reassurance as he did medicine. It was great to sit around and exchange ideas and theories and acknowledge that we are on a frontier here on so many levels, and how wonderful it is to be a part of it.

I am going to do my meditation and my grateful exercises, and then the mind-reach to Mark and fill him in on what has been happening with me.

We don't get much news of what is happening anywhere else, so I think we will draw a good crowd tomorrow, if for nothing else but the sake of curiosity and something different to do than shovel rubble or pound nails. I have not seen anyone else from our little group back here at the airport, so I think I am first to bed down, which is always a good thing because I don't have to make small talk about my day.

We have the big group meditation, and then it is my understanding that people will be heading over to Atlantis. It is just so odd to write that or to think that there is this huge continent that has risen and on the continent are roads and buildings and I heard someone say today there are some standing statues and an amphitheater and many larger buildings. It is so fascinating, and I am glad to be going myself. Nothing like facing the dragon head on and trying to stand up for what you believe at a time you think is crucial in history. This is certainly a unique time in history. This is the first time in hundreds of years that new land has been discovered, and as I have written before - since it rose out of the water we don't have to kill anyone to possess it. Here is hoping no one kills another over the new land.

I am going to wrap with the thought that this odyssey has to have an end, and surely I am near to it.

I am up early, and with no coffee I have decided to sit and do a little writing in my same spot from yesterday and then take a little walk about. It was not a restful night for me, with a lot of tossing and turning. I have a nervous energy I want to walk off and I am not looking forward to another flight over water. I am going to take advantage of how clear the roads are and go farther afield than I normally would and use that time to center and ground myself before the meditation with Leah this morning. I don't remember my dreams, and it felt like Reginald and I were the only ones tossing and turning. The others got in much later and slept heavily. I enjoy taking these moments to reflect on the craziest days of my life so far, and it is not yet over. I wonder how an ordinary someone like me has ended up with this group of movers and shakers. I feel that my fellow doctors were showing me a different kind of respect because of my intensity about this energy stuff once I got going, and maybe because I had tried to put it into practice. Admittedly, once I told them the story of Neil I monopolized the conversation. I could feel the energy running through me as I talked about what doctors could be in the future, and at one point I mentally asked for guidance from the other side to be able to communicate my ideas properly and intuitively told them about the discarnate souls on the other side.

The idea of discarnate souls that have greater knowledge on the other side who are tasked with working with an incarnate soul on Earth as it muddles through life appeals to me more than praying to a distant god who has so many people to look after. It makes more sense that we all are working together on both sides to achieve the oneness instead of being "down here" and being judged for our bad behavior or being "up there" somewhere and being home free. I don't know how I personally feel about being absorbed into a large consciousness, but I am sure that is just how I perceive it in my limited human way.

I am up and off on the walkabout. It was always one of my favorite things when traveling to get up early and walk around. A place will give up all its secrets early in the morning. I think maybe I have started to view this like a trip to a foreign country. I think I am picturing Atlantis like the ruins of ancient Greece, when really it sounds like the buildings are in decent shape. It is hard to imagine what it is going to be like and what we are going to do when we get there. I must admit to feeling a bit of longing to see it. I cannot figure out if the longing stems from wanting all of this to be over or from wanting to see and be on the continent itself. Part of the tossing and turning last night had to do with vivid, fragmented images of Atlantis coming and going each time I fell into restful sleep. I think it was the images that dredged up that longing, which continues to linger on me like soap residue this morning.

I am off to see what there is to be seen and grab some water for my freeze-dried egg breakfast, and if I am lucky I might score some coffee.

11:20 a.m.

I don't know how many times I can really write that I have been amazed. When will I accept this stuff as part of everyday reality? The meditations and the question-and-answer session about Atlantis were illuminating and beyond any group meditation yet. I am excited and at peace at the same time. Many of my nagging questions have been answered.

I had a great walk around town. There are such differences here. The streets are patrolled night and day by military, which is understandable because the general was camped at a state forest near the reinforced bunker where Ian and Isolde's parents and who knows which other high-level government and military officials were staying. That put the officials and their families on the run for the first few days when they were all here together and made them feel more insecure, which probably adds to that divisive energy I felt.

The general was smart, it seems. He had his people gather supplies and arms in places such as Denver and on the West Coast, where there was not much military strength or organization, and grouped and doubled his force here to put everyone on edge, with the full plan of heading to Atlantis to explore this great power source. He wants to be first to it so that he ensures things are done the way he wants them done. I am beginning to wonder if he is an enemy or an ally against elected leadership. As Reginald pointed out, he at least presents another option. Without him it would be business as usual, with the same few people making decisions for whatever majority of us is left. Those decisions may or may not be what is right for this new environment.

Now people know of a second and even a third option – the cooperative town hall. I think there are so few of us now that we can all have a say in how we want things to go if there is a huge new continent to be set up. The people of the world have something wonderful to focus on, and Atlantis sounds pretty wonderful.

Jon gave a concise description of what happened at the Mid Regional summit to those gathered for the mediation, and then Leah led the large group meditation. The way she was able to link everyone in so quickly and smooth the linked-group mind was a bit startling.

After the meditation, she gave what she described as a history lesson about Atlantis. The continent was in existence after the Ice Ages and had formed in the same way and had been populated in the same way as the other continents had, thousands and thousands of years ago.

She said the difference between development of the people of Atlantis and that of other indigenous peoples on other continents had to do with the immense deposits of natural quartz crystal scattered all over the continent of Atlantis. The crystal was used by the people for personal decoration, tools, building and also became a part of every aspect of their every day lives. Quartz crystal has six primary functions of which the people unintentionally took advantage initially, so the Atlantis society developed differently. The six uses of quartz crystal are structure, store, amplify, focus, transmit and transform energy, which includes matter, thought, emotion and information. The crystals were integrated into everything the indigenous people did and became an integral part of their culture. The people began noticing how the crystals worked on harmonizing and bolstering energy of all types. Things really developed over successive generations, and soon Atlantean people had jumped ahead of surrounding indigenous people culturally, technologically and, most importantly, spiritually -- so much so that they had to cut off ties and trade with the surrounding peoples of the world.

Atlantis became a completely self-sustaining continent, and its people became very spiritually advanced and well-versed in using the crystals. The society was so advanced it sounds unreal. Travel was free because there were anti-gravity aircraft that everyone learned to fly like riding a bike when they were very young. Most people were self- sufficient, but those who could not or did not want to be self-sufficient were cared for. Atlanteans did not have a monetary system in place because they had evolved past needing money as a form of exchange. They shared generously with one another and bartered when they had to. There was a no-harm rule on Atlantis; no person was allowed to lay hands on another in a violent way or with violent intent. Civic responsibility started in the home at birth and developed from there. Every single person was involved in government, so they all had investment in how things were run. There was no competition with each other for success. The competition was with oneself, a striving to be the very best at whatever it was you were engaged in.

It was a society of contemplation. The people spent at least twenty-five percent of their time in meditation, and some people spent up to seventy percent of their time in spiritual contemplation. This eventually led to the society thinning out physically because as they developed spiritually, they forgot to check in physically, and the population diminished over generations.

Finally, a great deluge broke the continent apart and created a main continent with outlying islands. At that point, it became harder to keep the other cultures out. Others soon found and set foot on the islands of Atlantis, which had not happened for generations. Missionaries from Atlantis had visited other cultures to try to bring them up to speed, but the Atlanteans had in the past erected an incredible mind barrier that kept anything and everything away from the continent. At that point the people of Atlantis began to want to have interaction. They were coming back from the spiritual inclination and wanting to experience the physical. They were falling in love with people from outside Atlantis. Legends of Atlantis began growing in other cultures, more people were finding the continent and integrating, and it was inevitable that other cultures would want the crystals and other items of value the Atlanteans possessed. Atlanteans had the no-harm rule in place for themselves and for visitors as well, so there were no defensive measures to guard people and valuables. Soon, the foulest of all offences was being committed in the islands. There began violent invasion's and people were being killed for their possession's.

Atlanteans had decisions to make as a population. Were they going to let themselves be invaded, their population killed off and the crystals scattered far and wide by people who had no idea how to use them? They could have tried to quickly educate people about how to use the crystals or they could protect the crystal technology until a time the world as a whole was ready to use it. They decided as a population that the people, the crystals, the technology and everything would have to be protected and the only way to do that completely and with the least amount of harm to everyone involved was to secure the valuables underground, evacuate the entire population of Atlantis -- and sink the continent.

It was not a decision entered into lightly, but they decided it was the only way. The process of securing and evacuating took many months to complete, and when everyone was settled on their new continents, at a designated time and from different locations around the world there was one last mind link to submerge Atlantis. The sinking was more powerful than any thought it would be, and created a worldwide flood that destroyed much more than they thought it would. That flood is the reason so many cultures have the same flood story.

The people of Atlantis had assimilated into other cultures, and some were killed by the very flood they created. Few met with huge success, really. They had thought they would be able to keep the mind-reach alive, but without being together, trying to work within cultures that were not advanced and not having the crystals as intermediaries, they were not able to maintain it. They had made the decision to secure or bury all of the crystals in an all-or-nothing approach.

Leah explained that a lot of the god mythology came about at this time when the Atlanteans left their continent and assimilated into other cultures worldwide. Some also chose to settle previously uninhabited lands such as Norway, or not settle at all and become the gypsies of legend. Some thrived and some died out quickly. They were never able to show the world what they had achieved, because if they showed off too much they were distrusted and killed. They were never as able to be free as they were on their home continent.

They knew there would come a time that Atlantis would rise again and the world would be different and more ready to use the crystals and technology. Most vowed they would reincarnate at that time and make their way back, or somehow make sure the entire world would have access to the harmony the crystals brought.

There are several large crystals and a Hall of Crystal that helps link all, but it is not as if you can just show up and power them up and have the technology up and running overnight. Then there are the thousands upon thousands of smaller crystals that were used for everything from meditation to healing to growing crops. Besides the crystals, there were rare metals and jewels. The people had learned to grow gems and used them for their decorative arts. It was a society where people valued the very best of everything. It was a competition to be the best, but it was a race for a personal best. Anything and everything one engaged in was given full attention and striving to make as perfect as possible. From growing the best tomato to being the best out-of-body traveler, the goal in life was to make it amazing.

Everything on Atlantis could be called amazing, Leah said. There was beauty everywhere one turned, and limitless abundance.

Now we are getting ready to go over there ourselves. We will fly over in about an hour. Leah will guide us to the center of the continent, well away from the general.

We had an unexpectedly large turnout for the meditation and the history lesson about Atlantis, and I was surprised to see as many military as were there. People asked some interesting questions about the crystals. Mainly, people were nervous that there was a huge power source that someone without the best of intentions could find and use it to do harm to others. Leah said that anyone could find one of the larger crystals but there would be no way they could find the Hall of Crystal, which links all the biggest crystals. Even if they did, she said, the crystals have to be worked with and attuned and powered back up before they can be used again for anything. Even then, it would be hard to use the crystals to do harm. Crystals promote harmony and peace, and have that effect on people when they are around them. If anything, the crystals would work to calm and soothe any warlike impulses any of the military contingents could be feeling. Everyone was answering the old call back to Atlantis, Leah said, and the militaries from other countries and the general are just a few. All have unfinished business that needs to be completed.

The militaries of several other countries apparently have landed on the new continent, and every nation has expressed an interest in having a presence there. Leah said we should be so excited about this prospect. This is a perfect time for people of the world to come together at the same time to build this back to what it was as a world instead of one distinct civilization that was so far advanced among those who were not. It's a chance to use that advanced technology to help rebuild the world that much more quickly.

It is exciting to think of a world at peace that has that no violence but lots of beauty and technology. I saw a bumper sticker once that said, "Why do we always have money for war but not for education?" If a society and a world spent all their resources on education and did not have to spend money to defend themselves from one another, what a nice world it would be. What a nice world it would be if money and fear did not exist.

Someone asked about the money because Leah said there was no money exchange on Atlantis. She explained how a barter system was in place, and many temples and places of worship always provided for the indigent or those choosing spiritual contemplation. No one went hungry or homeless on Atlantis, she said, and the food and shelter were abundant and beautiful. There were riches beyond measure, so there was no competition for wealth, since spirituality and not the compiling of wealth was the goal of their society. If there was competition it was for spiritual aptitude, and in that vein people were eager to help one another and give to one another because it advanced themselves and everyone spiritually. People on the receiving end did their best in everything they did.

How to treat total strangers with love and generosity? Everyone on Atlantis was pretty much a cousin, and if every person you ever met was family I can see how everyone would take care of one another. People lived in great family cooperatives. There were stationary clans and travelling clans and everything in between. The bottom line was that people loved one another on Atlantis. There was not divisiveness and fear, and no concern for one's own personal safety at all times.

Because they were so advanced, they knew there would

be great civilizations that would rise and fall but that one day there could be a balance where there was peace throughout the world and all cultures worked together toward it.

As Leah talked about this, she fairly glowed with light. It was as if she became ethereal right before our eyes. Her longing was so palpable that all of us would have willingly done whatever it took to achieve that world peace right there.

I wondered what the plan would be once we all started landing on the shores, and thankfully someone else asked the question out loud. Most of the buildings are intact and we are welcome to settle in any of these anywhere on the continent once everyone has the lay of the land. As more sand shifts, we will find other buildings and entrances to underground facilities. All are dry and comfortable on the inside and there is plenty of room. Everything we will need to live is stored in underground caches all over the huge continent. The caches include food, dishes, utensils, furniture and everything else needed to set up households.

Leah will be pulling out the crystals and demonstrating how to use them. She laughed and said it would not just be her who knows where the crystals are and their functions. Anyone can get to them and begin working with them, she said, and soon Atlantis will be a place of pilgrimage for holy people and regular people who have a holy leaning. It will draw people like a magnet. There will be no stopping the influx of people coming back to settle Atlantis.

Someone wondered about the military, and at this point Reginald again strode to the front of the room. You can tell he felt distaste in having to assume a leadership role. He gave a speech about his long involvement with the military and achieving rank, and said that he personally wanted to set down arms and hoped it would never again get to a point that a conflict would require arms. He put forth the theory that military personnel across the board, from leadership all the way down to the last corps member, might have to decide this thing, not the elected leadership or the general. Reginald's take was that the military people might just have to take a big vote about how they want this to proceed, and he said that setting down arms would be his suggestion.

When we get there, our group plans to set up huge white flags to indicate we are at peace in this land and go to great lengths to work with the general and his group to bring them on board. We ask other countries that if they send military, let it be as representatives of their people until the regular people can be ferried over as well. Other nations already seem amenable as well to having this continent be a no-weapons and no-harm-done zone until we can work out the logistics. Most countries have not put the issue to a vote to find what their people want to do.

I myself wonder what we will do when we get over there, but when the question was put to Leah she smiled and said something like, "You will see what you shall see and find plenty to keep you occupied." There were questions about things like, "What does ten thousand-year-old food taste like?" and Leah said there would be dried food of every variety that is quite edible, and there are seeds stored from which we could have fresh produce within eight months. With the caches of food that had been stored all over the United States, we would have more than enough supplies to bridge until we could literally begin to feed the world.

Then there was the show-and-tell portion. A few of the crystal tablets were passed around, and a slide show was played to reveal what Atlantis had physically looked like -- and it looked magical. People asked how they could be seeing pictures of Atlantis if it had not been around for thousands of years, and she explained that these crystal tablets stored all sorts of valuable information in addition to being communication devices, and that these pictures had been taken on Atlantis when it was still above the water. She had powered up the tablets to show slides, she said, and explained they were fairly common and we would all use them and other types of crystals in our daily lives for everything from communication to growing our backyard gardens. They are beautiful in form and clarity, and just holding them and watching them display the images is proof that there was advanced technology.

I did not hold one of the tablets because I did not want to be tempted to try to look for Mark and the babies again and either disrupt the process or break down blubbering in the middle of the session. When I glanced over the shoulders of people who were holding the tablets, I could see picture-postcard views of landscapes of all types. I did not see any people or animals in any of the pictures, and I wondered if the images had been captured as the evacuation was taking place.

To end the show-and-tell session, Leah called the two wolfhounds to the front of the room. They looked resigned as they padded forward and sat down at her feet -- and even more resigned as she levitated them. When they had risen about six feet into the air they stopped as if sitting on a platform and then suddenly sat up on their hind legs and threw their front paws into the air in an imitation of the kind of cheer a person would do when their favorite team scores. The sight was so funny that the crowd roared with laughter. The wolfhounds looked sheepishly pleased as they were lowered, and scampered off once they touched the ground. All tension in the room was broken, and Leah talked about using energy in all sorts of new ways and how the unusual will be the new usual. She stressed again that to use the power, good intent has to be there and the crystals are actually powered most strongly by group energy. Family units were strong on Atlantis for many reasons, she said, and it is that love that really powers the crystals, in addition to the energy that flows on Atlantis.

Then she said something that made all of us cheer and want to go to Atlantis. She said that once we get over there, we may be able to get some rays of sun to break through.

Reginald is going to suggest that a vote by all branches of the military take place tomorrow. He is not proposing the vote as some sort of final stand, instead just getting a read on the feelings of a large cross section of people that happen to be most directly involved with any decision that is made. He suggested doing the vote by felt cloth so it will be anonymous. He thought one branch of service should run the vote and another monitor the outcome, and that the result would be a good indication of how actual military people would wish to proceed.

We are still using one of the radios to monitor communication and stay in touch with DIA. There is still no word from the general about why he is on Atlantis or what he proposes to do there. Announcements from DIA that broadcast peace to the general and to anyone else in the world that might be listening are going every three hours. There is a quick broadcast of developments from DIA to keep anyone who cares to listen in the loop.

We are still not getting much response from the highest leadership in the land, and I realize that has something to do with the status of Isolde and Ian's family and the fact that leadership might be undecided about all of this and not wanting a part of it. Then I have a thought that they are going to stay in one place and see if the common people would fight it out with the general if that is what it takes, and once that path is cleared, they will be able to organize and safely lead the regular military right on in to what is left.

I never realized that these underground structures on the East Coast and probably everywhere else were so extensive. They have their own reservoirs and air-filtration systems, and are well stocked with every kind of ration. The one near where we landed has a chamber big enough that the entire Congress can meet together, which is probably what has been happening since the catastrophe. Many will be able to live comfortably for long periods of time down there.

I just want things to be open and not shadowy. From the sound of Atlantis and feeling the new energy myself, it sounds like it is going to be a brilliant new world. I am excited to get over there, see it for myself and feel the energy up close. It seems the pull grows stronger for me by the moment, but I also think I am now tuning in with Isolde and Bea and Leah more closely. The three of them are beside themselves to be going over there this afternoon, and none of them plans on returning.

We have not exactly stirred the crowd as we hoped to do here. It's partly because the population seems more apathetic here and partly because we have to coordinate flights to the new continent with the military. While they are not exactly blocking the effort, there is a lot of talk about fuel supplies. We don't know where it is located or where we could go to find large amounts, so we have asked them for enough to get at least our groups from Denver over and they have agreed to that. I think they almost want us out of the way so that we don't get things too stirred up. I think they are hoping we make our way to the new continent and get taken out by the general and his militia.

Not much input from the West Coast. The representatives they have on the radio say clearing is going well. They are so hard hit that the last thing on their minds seems to be trying to travel to the new continent or who will be running things there.

I wondered as well if we were going to run into direct conflict on Atlantis and talked with Ian a little about it. He gave his usual disclaimer that there is danger in every step one takes in the world, and that is the reason to always be on alert and trusting intuition. However, he is positive there is not going to be any sort of combat over there, just big discovery and adventure. I was reassured to hear that he thought it was going to be an adventure and not a struggle for dominance.

I don't need to repack the pack. We stocked up before we left DIA, so my pack is ready to go. It is amazing how that pack has turned into the anchor of my little world. Hopefully this will be my last stop before I return to South Park. There is irony in the fact that I keep writing that and then traveling farther away.

It is amazing to think that the next time I write I will be on ground that has not been exposed to air in more than ten thousand years. If Isolde's theory is true, I lived lifetimes on Atlantis and the reason I am feeling this stuff so strongly and why I am directly involved is because I was directly involved back then in the decision and follow-through on the sinking of Atlantis.

What if I was someone who actively campaigned for it among my peers? Part of my mission in this life may be to help lead people back there to make it what it was and make it available to the world.

Our group plans to set up camp right in the middle of the continent. There is a small cluster of buildings that is near a medium-sized amphitheater, and from there we will explore, find the caches of crystals and begin bringing them on line. To do that, we will place the crystals in specific locations where they vibrate at their highest frequency and then focus our meditations upon them.

Leah is a little vague about instruction on how to work everything. She says the instructions are built into the crystals, and different people will be able to access the ways to work things at different times as their skills develop. There are no instructions written down on paper about how to fly an anti-gravity glider if we happen to come across one. Nor are there buttons and switches on any of the devices that would enable them to be figured out. Leah said it will be a little like strangers in a strange land as we are drawn to specific crystals and become familiar with them and begin to work with them until we figure out how they operate.

I have heard that the flight over the ocean is no cakewalk, and I am not looking forward to it. Thankfully the new continent is only about one hundred and twenty miles offshore, so the trip will not be as long as the flight from Denver to the East Coast was and the prospect of seeing the sun makes the trip more appealing.

6:24 p.m.

Here we are, settled on Atlantis.

That seems like a line from a movie instead of something I would ever write in my journal. The ride over in the plane was not as bad as I thought it would be. I think we were holding the plane steady with our minds, but I can never be sure.

I am beginning to trust this new energy and can feel the resonating vibration now that I am on Atlantis. I feel so happy here. It does feel like I have returned after a great while.

We flew a large convoy over and set up camp as a group. The camp has the same feel that Civic Center did, except that we have intact buildings. There are buildings and roads still in place, and they are beautiful. The roads are in good shape, and it is strange to fly over a continent and see clear roads, standing buildings and no rubble. The material the roads are made of reminds me of that advanced material they have for the kids to fall on at the playgrounds these days, but more tightly woven and harder packed.

We landed in a long field and I wondered what it had looked like back in its heyday. The land looks like dried-out beach. There are no trees or foliage, which gives it the feel of a moonscape without the pitting. Leah says to stick to the roads because there are still some areas that are dangerous, but it is not like we have to worry about wild animals running loose. We know where the general is, and we are doing a group meditation tonight that specifically reaches out to his group to try to get a mind-link. They are hundreds of miles away on a coast, camped in a cave they believe to be the gateway to the Hall of Crystal. Leah said it is indeed a gateway to the Hall of Crystal, but it is one of many and the general will spend a lot of time trying to figure out how to get in. She says that time he is spending is good for him and his crew.

Leah hung out with us for about two hours as we all got our spaces set up. She answered questions and gave us all a crystal to begin meditating with. She let us know she would love to do a group meditation with us early tomorrow morning, beginning at the exact time of sunrise, and that is when we will see her next and also those rays of sun. Then she disappeared over the horizon with Rue and the other dogs, almost skipping in her glee to be back and walking around freely. I can't wait to do a little exploring myself. Since we have landed, it is like my spirit is reveling in this energy that feels so light and joyous and seems to dance around in the air here. I feel like a kid on the first day back at my favorite summer sleep-away camp.

The rugs and furnishings had been set up in our buildings and are far nicer than anything one would find at sleep-away camp, and the crystals Leah gave out are beyond description, they are so beautiful. They are many different shapes, sizes and colors. Mine is a light amber color with a golden light inside that I think would nicely reflect the rays of the sun. It is round and a bit smaller than a baseball. It is cool to the touch and perfectly smooth, yet interactive in a way.

Leah also passed around a bunch of musical instruments, so we plan on having the sing-along after the meditation with Isolde tonight. The musicians in the camp were raving about the look and feel and sound of the instruments and seemed very excited to begin playing them together. I feel like everything has kind of come full circle. There are some people here from the original Civic Center camp and some DIA people in addition to our original seven and Consuela, so I have familiar people about, and that always makes me feel more comfortable. Everyone feels the lightness and has great expectations for what we can do here, and I have not heard a single serious discussion about the general.

Tomorrow we plan to do the sunrise meditation with Leah at the amphitheater nearby. Ian, Jon and some others are going to do a low flyover in the cargo plane today to see if we can spot the emissaries of the other countries so we can invite them over. We want the general to see the cargo plane and know where we are camping. I am sure he knows of all the comings and goings so far. We have had two huge white squares painted on either side of the plane since Brush to indicate the white flags of peace, and we put our giant white flags up immediately upon arrival at the residences.

At the meditation tonight, we will be mind-reaching the general's group and inviting them to our meditations. We think they have to be developing some group mind-link of their own and surely have realized the energy has lightened and that there are crystals here that amplify and magnify all the light energy.

I have not done much concentrating or reaching for the brutish member of that group during my meditations. I think that is a good thing in that I am not thinking of him or being frightened of being near him and his group and what they might have represented. I have developed a surprising indifference, and at this point I am feeling pity for the brutish one, wondering what his background must have been to cause him to need to lash out and try to dominate and control his environment. I am glad to know he is experiencing this light energy because I know it cannot help but lighten his spirit.

I get the feeling we perhaps are re-enacting the original standoff. Maybe the general and his followers, in past lives, were the group that was invading and killing people to steal the crystals, jewels and other valuables. The Atlanteans decided to sink the continent rather than let the invaders kill to get what they wanted, and that decision had its own repercussions, so now we have all come back to let it play out as it should have back then.

The general is back, with access to the crystals. Many of the past Atlanteans are back also with full access to the crystals and saying, "Let's do this differently this time." It is not right to fight for resources but it is not right to try and hide them away and keep knowledge from others either. This is the point in time where we find the balance, and perhaps we are meeting back up to find the resolution.

I am bunking with Isolde, Ian and our little group in what was a residence. It has several different rooms, one of which is a bathroom that looks like it had running water. It is cozy, but the rooms are well laid out and this place and all the buildings here have very high ceilings, which makes everything feel more spacious. The building material is also a little like that playground material, but more substantial in a way, and a beautiful mellow white color with inlaid mosaics. The residences are clumped near one another, and what must have been the main gathering buildings and the temples are right in the center. All roads lead to or perhaps begin at these main gathering places, whether they are at the center or the outskirts of the residences. It seems the houses were small and the main gathering places were huge because they spent a significant amount of time together in the larger group spaces or in meditation together, or in meditation spaces outside or at the temples.

As we flew in, you could see the layouts of towns and fields. I did not see any larger developments that indicated cities. We flew over a small barrier ring of islands to land on the main continent. From what I understand the surrounding islands might have been larger long ago but now they resemble low-lying keys, like the Florida Keys. I guess that is what a few thousand years of erosion on the bottom of the ocean will bring.

Crystals are stored in caches on those islands and on the mainland. There are large and small crystal caches in various locations on all continents, above and below ground. Many are on Atlantis, but the past Atlanteans also scattered them on other continents for protection and future access. We will begin unearthing and setting them up tomorrow. Leah is going to show us one of the big caches right after the group meditation, so we get a chance to see how they were stored and what a group of them looks and feels like together, and then we will start bringing them up and out of storage. They should begin responding immediately to our energy, and then we begin to practice using them.

On Atlantis, certain crystals were developed by certain families or cooperative units. A specialization of sorts happened when those who had an affinity for a certain type of crystal begin to work with that crystal to its best advantage. The crystal in turn becomes more powerful because it is being worked at its highest potential. Crystals shore up the energy of people who work with them and hold the energy, so crystals were placed with the family units or groups that could best develop them. For instance, if there was a healing-energy crystal, it would be stored in the home of a specialist in medicine or meditated upon by a family or group of healers. After a time in the home, or after being meditated upon for a time, the healing energy is stored by the crystal. The crystal can then be transferred to the healing center, where it is placed near an ailing patient who can then meditate upon the same crystal and draw the healing energy, which is magnified by the crystal as it is drawn. All things are full circle, and it is a win on so many levels. The meditation on all sides is energizing and healing, as is the working together as a people with good intent. Being able to spend a considerable amount of time in meditation is a win on its own levels so all of it is intrinsic.

For many years, as the Atlanteans were developing their group energy, they used the skills they were developing to harmonize and then simply to keep people out. They would create images of impenetrable rock barriers or sea monsters surging from the waters around the continent so sailors either could not find a place to land or sailed the other way in a hurry. The very few who did make it to Atlantis rarely left. Occasionally someone who had come via shipwreck could not live without their own family, and that person would be taken and gently placed back with his people. The punishment for someone who flouted the rules of Atlantis in the beginning was banishment to another culture that was more fitting to that crime and personality. Never mean, the Atlanteans insisted the criminal be dropped with plenty of wealth to live comfortably, and certainly also had uncommon skills with which to make a living.

The Atlanteans were artists, writers, metal workers, scientists, every profession and every walk of life. They all had the same desire to learn about their world and how to live in it as we do today. They were delighted with technology but got their greatest joy when everything was for the greatest good. The guy who could grow the most fantastic wheat crop was proud to have extra to give to his neighbors and have them compliment the fine quality. When the neighbors' child did something extraordinary, you were so proud of that kid and happy for the accomplishment because you knew that youngster would be furthering society. If everyone is treating everyone else well, all are assured of good treatment. Amazing how that worked.

After the meditation and sing-along, I plan on wandering and doing my personal meditation out in the open tonight. It is always good to be camping indoors because it gives the clothing and socks a chance to dry, so I don't mind getting a little more damp than usual. I want to see if my center feels stronger here to match the peaceful feeling I have been getting of having returned to a place I loved so much. I want to do my first work with my crystal out in the open as I meditate. I want my first mind-reach to Mark to be undiluted by restrictive walls or any sort of interruption.

I got some herbal tea from Beatrice, so I am going to head for the central gathering place and enjoy some tea and fellowship before the meditation and sing-along. A part of me was hoping to trade the tea for some coffee because I want the caffeine, but Beatrice read my thoughts as she handed me the tea and laughed and told me she had formulated this blend just for me and wanted me to drink it and not trade it for coffee. She explained that as an herbalist she does more than blend a bunch of leaves together. As she makes a blend she is focused on who she is blending for and what she wants that mixture to do for them. Because she knows I can't eat for a few hours after a plane ride, she has a stomach soother and energizing herbs, but it is also the energy that is inherent in the blend. It is not just the physical tea she makes; it is also the energy she puts into it as she thinks of me.

11:20 p.m.

It was a beautiful night. Isolde feels more relaxed now that she is here and I think I could feel it in her meditation. This group seems to have the hang of how to check in to meditate since the guided meditation with Leah -- or maybe we are all taking advantage of the light energy in the air. We were all able to link in and form a strong connection quickly. There was no dissonance and I could actually feel the organic presence of my own crystal and maybe the others as well, since everyone is now carrying their crystal everywhere. In a funny way, it reminds me of the "pet rock" craze as we show one another our crystals, admire those of others and speculate on the use and concentration of energy that the crystal will channel best.

When we focused on the general and his group, we got a clear picture of them this time. They are camped comfortably in a cave that they are using as headquarters, and also have people stationed all over the island. They have freed many crystals and are working with them. They are working with their own group energy, and I got a strong impression they are focusing on mathematical formulas as the way to solve a puzzle or open a door. The most interesting things about doing the mind-connect with them was hearing the background music and the way they opened up to us but blocked us at the same time when they felt us. It is a palpable thing. When we were reaching out to them as a group, I personally could feel their feeling us and putting up a mental barrier. They also have music in their minds and on their minds. They are still heavily armed but don't seem mentally attached to their guns and weapons. Maybe the guns were more for show so they were not challenged by anyone else. They have a big cross section of people, and all of them feel strongly that they are right about being here and what they are doing, which seems to be trying to get to the Hall of Crystal.

I was not able to make a connection to the brutish one, nor was I able to ever get the general. They clearly feel that it is their mission to get to this great power source so they can control it. They are growing strong with their mind-link as they work with the crystals. I did not get the feeling of fanaticism or violent intent, just the solid feeling that they were convinced they were right, had a mission and were not going to be swayed.

During the sing-along, many people came into camp. During the flyover today Ian and Jon found and talked with several camps that ended up coming on over and made it in time for the sing-along.

We are going to have to get some smaller planes soon. These huge jets come rumbling over, and it feels like an international airport -- or maybe I am not used to the noise anymore after many days of nothing in the airspace above.

There was a wonderful moment when a traveler from DIA was talking to someone from their home country who landed on Atlantis from a cruise ship wreck during the aftermath of the storm. It turns out they had gone to the same university and had many mutual friends. It was a very roundabout, coincidental connection, but it seemed that these connections were going to be happening in the future as par for the course when everyone began to come together.

There was a reaching out to the people who joined the camp that I was so happy to see. Everyone wanted to make the connection and welcome others, and the people who had been camped on Atlantis to stake the claim for their country or who landed in the storm were so happy to see travelers who are coming in peace instead of a huge military force.

The sing-along was a favorite part of the evening for me, as usual. There were many old favorites to be sung, and we learned some new songs from the people from other cultures who joined us. I think one of the songs we were taught by some foreign soldiers might have been a bawdy double-entendre song because they could not contain their laughter when a few of us repeated some of the verses after they sang them. The instruments played beautifully, and there was some dancing.

There were sad moments interspersed. Someone began a folk song about leaving people you love, and we stopped the sing-along after that one and dedicated the moment in time to all the wonderful people we had lost who would have loved to have been there and should have been there at that moment. We rejoiced with them in spirit.

It was then I understood how close the Other Side really is. I always think of those in spirit as far-away distant and removed from us, but I could feel them there in droves, celebrating with us. They are on a non-physical plane, but they have access to wherever they want to be at any given time in physical reality and in realms that we cannot conceive, and they are so happy that we are waking up and recognizing them and opening to their help.

It was a good meditation, and I have a strong feeling that

we are going to be able to rebuild to that utopian society faster than I thought might be possible as long as we can get the general and the leaders and the military and other countries on board. The military representatives from the other countries are the same as us. They too want to organize and rebuild as soon as possible and live in a world of peace, whether here or back in their own countries. Life is so precious, and we have all been through so much, the last thing I can imagine is to fight one another over a piece of land or what god one prays to. They have been warned about the general and know he is here to go after the power source. We all just wish he would make contact and let us know his intentions, or at least agree to lay down his weapons.

Later in the evening I set off on my own and found a small round gazebo-like structure about fifty feet off the road. The sand looked hard packed enough to risk, and as I walked toward it I got the impression it was once in a grove of trees. There were built-in alcoves that had to have been for crystals, and I instinctively put my crystal in one and faced the direction I intuited was best. My energy was somehow synching to the general energy I feel on Atlantis -- the collective energy, as it were. I unrolled a little carpet I brought that was in one of the rooms of the residence for us. It is a beautiful red and purple and must also have had metal thread woven in that glimmered as I unrolled it. I did the meditation on my knees with my hands joined and crossed over my heart instead of in the crossed-leg position. I centered myself and chanted "Yod Hey Vah Hey" for a while until my thoughts were very still. I was at ease and more relaxed than I thought I would be. I feel so comfortable here, as if I have come into me. I feel also as if I am being welcomed by the energy, or as if the sprites of Atlantis are spinning around me in delight.

I did the mind-reach with Mark and told him all about what I have been participating in and what my feelings about it have been. Tonight the mind-reach was more like a conversation, and it felt as if he was aware that I was reaching out to him and communicating with him. I could feel the rustle of excitement when I checked in, and then he held the energy for the full time. I was beside myself with delight, of course. His energy feels as it always does. His energy has always felt warm and open and caring, with a strong dash of happy-go-lucky.

After my meditation I still was not feeling tired, so I decided to take a little walk down one of the side roads leading away from the pagoda. Even though it is still raining and the moon is not visible, I was enjoying my trek alone in the dark, which is unusual for me because I am not one to enjoy walking in an unknown place in the dark. My head lamp was barely cutting the dark and I was wearing my backpack out of habit, so I was not moving quickly. I walked along and began to feel Reginald's thoughts echoing at the edges of mine and I know he felt my mind as I sensed he was ahead. I speeded up my steps and he slowed his down, and all of a sudden I got a strong past-life impression of running to meet my twin because we had something serious to talk about. I realized Reginald and I had experienced a past life together as twins in the last days of Atlantis; we had campaigned for the sinking of the continent.

I was glad to see him, and since we don't have to verbalize much I threw him the quick mind-thought of being twins in that past life on Atlantis and campaigning for the sinking of the continent and I could feel his mind do an ah-hah!

He told me he was out walking because he had some things weighing on his mind. He said he feels the military was called out today after we had gone. It would have been the full call for active and non-active personnel, and even the old militia public call to arms that would take anyone who would volunteer to suit up. He said that if his intuitions are correct, the U.S. military will be sending a large force to the shores of Atlantis tomorrow. He is going to share this news with our group this evening and then with all gathered tomorrow at sunrise meditation. I was so angry, feeling that all we had done had been for naught. I was so angry that the military people would not choose to take a vote before they would decide to take up arms instead of laying them down, even after participating in the meditation and knowing what is at stake here on Atlantis.

Reginald picked up on that and told me I have to think of the military not as a large unthinking body who mindlessly follows but as regular people who are having many of the same thoughts about this as we are -- and yet they will answer the call to duty because that is what they committed to do when they signed up and that loyalty is what made our military and our nation what it was, which was one of the greatest countries in the history of Earth.

I was really disturbed by this news, but Reginald thinks this is a good thing. He would rather have this happening up front so we can get everything settled instead of later when everyone is comfortable and complacent.

I don't know how I am going to get any rest tonight thinking of a huge U.S. military force landing here tomorrow. Atlantis is going to be taken over and the energy corrupted. Even as I wrote that, I wondered if that is what the thinking was that led to the sinking of the continent in the first place. I guess it must play out this time as it will for all of us. It is a different time but it is the same situation rearing its ugly head, right as the continent resurfaces. The irony is that it was only postponed for ten thousand years.

I will be glad to get the bigger crystals out and on line. Better to have everything out in the open this time around. We can quickly learn how to work with them and then work together to rebuild the world and get everyone back to their loved ones instead of making this some big military standoff. I know Reginald had his wife and kids on his mind, although we can all take a cue from the children who are having the time of their lives and will remember this time differently than will the adults.

Reginald and I walked back together and looked for the rest of the housemates to share the news. Many people were still at the gathering, so Reginald let them know what his intuition was telling him. Since the U.S. military would be mobilizing, it would effectively postpone or eliminate the military voting on whether they wanted to pick up arms and answer the call.

We agreed to proceed as usual tomorrow and

acknowledge that any country has a right to bring a large contingent of people, in whatever capacity they want, and we knew Leah would agree. Everything will proceed as usual tomorrow, beginning with the meditation and then getting to a cache and freeing the crystals and artwork and furnishings and gems and precious metals and whatever else we want to bring out. None of us brought weapons to Atlantis, so from here on out we are going to have to use our minds and maybe some of the mind energy we have been working on as a group to get through this.

I need to try to get some sleep so I can be on my game tomorrow. I am also going to fall asleep thinking of Atlantis in those final days and meditate on what we could do differently that will yield a better outcome this time around.

Day 12 4:36 a.m.

I dreamed of the old Atlantis last night, and this morning I am left with a true longing to be back there at that time. It was so peaceful and beautiful and safe and serene, I awoke with tears streaming down my cheeks. I see why we would have wanted to protect it and protect that way of life instead of watching it be slowly disassembled before our eyes by people who had no idea what they were doing. The dream was not like the movie-quality dream I had about Isolde flying us around with that flashing green ring, this dream was more about impressions and deep feelings. I saw what the buildings looked like when inhabited and how alive the land was. I got an overall sense of such love for one other and the surroundings and happiness overlying everything. It seemed like it would be a place where one would be excited to wake up and go about the day because everything was so pleasant and everyone got to do whatever they desired or were passionate about. There was such a feeling of freedom in the air. I got a great idea of what we might be shooting for here -- not literally, of course.

Being on Atlantis now, I am leaning toward wanting to meditate all the time. I can see how the people then might not have been able to mount any effective defense except for hiding or throwing up a fake visual wall. In theory, we are going to undo what we did when we sank the continent. The catastrophe has happened again, and this time we are gathered here to heal the aftermath, open the crystals to the Earth and set the world up for peace this time around.

I am going to get ready to go over to the amphitheater. I am excited about the meditation and about seeing some rays of sun. And I am ready to face whatever is coming to a head here on

Atlantis and get it resolved peacefully this time around so we can all move forward.

It is not like I am nervous about my own country's military landing here and shooting everyone up or trying to engage the general. I know we have to have a presence here as other countries do, but I wish we did not have to bring such a large force. Or I wish we could have had a military revolt and they could have laid down arms, but I think Leah is right. Let as many people come here as fast as possible in whatever capacity they are able to arrive.

1:14 p.m.

What an interesting morning it has been, as usual.

The meditation this morning was glorious. We all got right down to business on the mind-link, and because Leah is such a strong facilitator the link was fast and strong. We all know how serious it is to learn how to work with the energy, and we all really wanted to see those rays of sun. The sun did break through, and we were all so thrilled when the light began to shine that a huge cheer went up and our group energy deepened at the feeling of accomplishment.

The U.S. military landed in force about an hour later.

We were trekking down a long road toward the cache when the first planes arrived. I could not believe how many military they have brought over. The United States is easily the largest force here, and I fear this will draw the ire of the other countries that have only small contingents so far.

The cache was amazing and beyond description. We had followed a long, narrow road away from the amphitheater for about two miles to a solitary temple-like building that sat on a rise. We could tell it had once been surrounded by gardens instead of residences or other buildings because there were still outlines of planting beds. Leah told us we would go inside and concentrate as a group to open the wall in the building that leads to the cache. To open the wall, she said, we would focus as a group while chanting Yod Hey Vah Hey. We would also be sending love to the crystals stored inside. We were a large and motley group and people were asking how long it would take and other questions, so it took a bit of time for there to be that group focus.

Leah guided the chant, and then linked our joined minds to what felt like a collective mind of some sort. It was organic and aware, but held no judgment. It felt as if we had literally gotten in touch with the crystals. There was a tinkling that I would describe as bells, but tinkling bells makes the tinkling noise sound too mundane. Then a light otherworldly music began to play at the outer edges of our minds, and before our eyes the wall covered with the finest mosaic on one side of the temple began to slide soundlessly to one side.

Before us was a wide, sweeping spiral staircase leading down. The stairway was lit, and the stairs were inlaid with mosaics and gemstones in flower and vine patterns. We lined up and proceeded down in an orderly fashion to the bottom of the stairway where there was a door that looked like something out of a Cold War advertisement for bunkers. It was huge and looked metallic, but it was no kind of metal I had ever seen before. We had to line up and, one by one, touch our palm anywhere on the door until every single person in our group had touched the door. That created quite a U turn and more chattering on the stairway. Once every man, woman and child had touched the door, it opened without a sound onto a narrow corridor that sloped downward toward what looked like a large, well-lit room. We were all jammed in and impatient at this point, so there was an audible murmur when we saw that we would have to go single file down the corridor.

Once we had all filed down the corridor and into the huge room at the end, we saw crystals, floor to ceiling, in every color. I felt that the crystals recognized that we were there and were happy to see us. It was as if they brightened or glimmered as each person stepped through the archway. The cacophony of energy grew greater as the room became more crowded. I don't know why I expected the crystals to be serene and unresponsive. They were stored in clear crystal cases that one would describe as a display case, but again the words "display case" bring to mind something too ordinary. I was particularly drawn to the amber- and sapphire-colored crystals in various shapes. The large room had numerous antechambers filled with other wonders, and we were free to roam and touch and look through whatever we wanted. These were items that had decorated public buildings on Atlantis. The public buildings were open to all, twenty-four hours a day and seven days a week. There were no such things as office buildings, although all settlements had large gathering buildings in the center that acted as administrative buildings. There were no huge metropolitan cities on Atlantis. They had sprawling compounds, always with the group gathering either in the center or at the very best place on the land. If the compound had a particularly lovely spot, then that is where a central gathering building would be erected so that everyone could enjoy it at any time. The loveliest spots were always public spaces.

After we had spent some time exploring the antechambers and exclaiming over everything, we began to remove the larger crystals back through the narrow passage, up the stairs and outside. The crystals Leah chose for us to bring out are tall and narrow, and could only be carried out one at a time by two people up the passageway and out the door and then up the spiral staircase. We had gotten about eighteen of these large crystals laid out on the road and in the field when we saw a remarkable sight. A thin, clear crystal pallet was being flown down the road by Leah. She looked like Aladdin riding a very large crystal carpet.

She said we had brought out enough for now and should start energizing them. One at a time, we began taking turns working with Leah and the crystal energy by trying to lift a crystal pillar with our mind, up and onto the crystal pallet Leah was flying. She would assist with an initial mind-link and then introduce the energy of the crystal and link in with it to start the exercise off. Initially, it was slow going. The idea was to try to lift and manipulate the pillar with our own energy, always with Leah's mind-link in the background, holding everything steady -- like a parent holding on to the seat of the bike as the child learns how to ride. Some people had a natural affinity for one or the other of the pillars and could lift that one or this one more easily. Each of us was able to get them off the ground, and those of us who were most efficient were able to get a pillar loaded onto the pallet. Then there was everything in between, which made the exercise funny to watch. It turned out to be a great way to energize the crystals and spend time getting to know one another. We could tell who was really new to all of this stuff and who had been doing meditations. There was no worry about harming the crystals because you cannot break or chip them or anything when working with them this low to the ground, and I am sure it is why Leah had us go one at a time, so she could make sure there were no accidents. It is not like they are these inanimate objects. You can feel them responding and magnifying and building the energy.

Leah took a couple of the kids on rides on the pallet, and then began disbursing the crystals. The pallet doesn't fly fast or zigzag dangerously. It hovers steadily about four inches from the ground when stationary, and when it was moving it would be two feet off the ground and moving about the speed and velocity of a slow golf cart. In turns, Leah loaded up a crystal and a few people and flew off to destinations that would be the best receptors for the different colors. For today, we are putting the crystals within a fifty-mile radius of the amphitheater. Some of them went into buildings and some were set out of doors on intricately worked stands that looked like they were built for them. The stands looked light and delicate but were made of the same otherworldly metal as the door to the chamber, and it took two people to lift them.

Once we got the crystals in place, everyone was to meditate nearby for a while so we could get them grounded. We chose the crystal we wanted to be near and Leah would load it up and get as many people as wanted to be near it on board. Off they would go.

I wanted to be near one of the sapphire crystals near

water, which was very unusual for me because I am more of a mountain person than a water person. It was very calming for me today to sit and tune in with the sapphire energy of the pillar as I looked out on the calm water of an inland lake. It is not like I could see a vista, because the rain is still very much present despite the sun rays breaking through this morning. I began a rhythmic chanting of the "Yod Hey Vah Hey" as I concentrated on the crystal and my meditation went deeper than I feel I have ever gone. It felt transcendent, as if I were participating in the meditation and yet out of my body at the same time. I could also feel the crystals grow stronger as we meditated with them, my personal crystal and the sapphire pillar linking with the other crystals that had been carried out. At first it was as if I could hear a whispering which turned into almost a singing as the crystals grew stronger with the live energy being poured in.

I was feeling so tuned in that I wanted to try to work with the energy physically. I decided to try to levitate on my own. I got into what I thought was the best position to keep the energy circulating. I sat loosely cross-legged with my hands joined and pressed against my heart. First I grounded myself to Earth, then I centered my energy at the base of my spine, then I visualized myself levitating, and finally I thought, "Well, here goes nothing," and I concentrated and focused -- and nothing happened. If anything, I felt heavy as a stone. I readjusted my posture and tried a second time with the same result and thought, "Well, maybe I am not ready." Then I decided to try once more by visualizing my cells tuning into the crystal energy on an organic level. I focused on the energy of the sapphire crystal first, and then pictured my cells recognizing the mineral energy of the Earth the crystal and I share. My body began to feel like it was lightening, and I was able to picture that light energy buoying my physical body. I fully concentrated on the lightness of the energy at a cellular level and that is how I was finally able to lift myself a couple of inches off the ground. But then I got too nervous, lost the focus and dropped back to the ground. I was beyond myself with exultation at this feat, and so grateful that I was able to feel that tuning in on a cellular level. It felt so pure, and now I just feel like anything in the world is possible. It made me want to shout about what I have accomplished from the rooftops and let others know that if I can do it, anyone can.

I got back onto the road and began heading back to the residence. The rain seems lighter now, which is really encouraging. In Denver it was a constant drizzle, and now I can safely describe it as a drizzle that is broken by long periods of heavy mist.

I ran into Beatrice when I was three-quarters of the way back to the residence, and she was also beaming from her meditation exercise. She had been meditating not far from what she felt is a larger underground cache, to which she had felt drawn. She said she detected it the moment she sat down and realized there were other crystals nearby that were waiting to tune up and tune in. She said she probably would be able to begin finding her own caches soon. When she began her meditation, she gathered the force of all the crystals, the pillars and those she felt in the underground cache and her personal crystal to help power her meditation and said she had experienced a breakthrough like nothing she had been able to achieve back on our continent before the catastrophe. She described an out-of-body experience that involved astral travel to another plane. It was funny that we had such parallel yet different-level spiritual experiences. I wondered if everyone on the continent was beginning to feel the spiritual effects of the crystals being out in the open and charged up. Beatrice said she will continue to show me how I could work with the new energy and attain levels I had never dreamed existed.

Beatrice was beautiful and effervescent after the catastrophe when I met her at Civic Center, and now here on Atlantis she is downright ethereal. Even I can visibly see her aura. I am beginning to be able to see others' auras as well, and I believe I am accurately reading thoughts much more quickly than I used to. I think in the past I relied on physical cues to help me get the read and now my mind is able to quickly check in and get the read right away. I can see how there would have been no crime on Atlantis. One would have been able to sense malicious intent from miles away. It would stick out like a sore thumb.

I think that is why I am not afraid with the U.S. military here that things are going to take a turn for the drastic where everyone starts shooting. I don't get the feeling that people can work that bad energy into a reality here -- not to mention the way every single one of us holds life dear at this point.

Beatrice was excited thinking her military buddies might be on Atlantis, and said she was going to head over to the mess hall the military had set up to look for them. For today, the army seemed determined to set up as many different small camps all over the continent as it could; this is unusual since most countries have only one large camp. Everyone seems to be taking this in stride, since any country has as much right as another to be here and the general has a few outposts set up here and there.

This is a free afternoon, and then we have the meditation at sunset tonight. I am hoping it is followed by the sing-along but I think we are going to introduce the ol' town hall format first. Jon is going to explain it to those gathered, since he has a succinct way of putting things.

As usual, the meditation, town hall and sing-along tonight will be open to anyone who wants to come. I know Leah has been cruising around on her pallet, encouraging people to show up even as she is helping energize the pillar crystals we put in place today and Ian is going around in the cargo plane letting everyone know we are here and wanting peace. Isolde is making rounds on foot, recruiting as many people as she can to the meditation, but I am beginning to realize that Ian and Isolde could have been flying their own pallets if they had wanted to. I think the three of them and Consuela have been working with crystals extensively throughout their lives and they can do far more and probably know far more than they are letting on.

I am starting to feel around the edges of the rest of our little group's minds because we have been working together so intensely. At any given time, I can kind of tune in with any member of our group, and their mind feels that I am there. I know this is happening because I can occasionally feel one or the other of them tuning into me at different times during the day, and when I have asked the person if they had tuned in with me at that time they answer affirmatively. This is being magnified greatly by the energy in the air and the very strong emotions of the people who are working with it. I think every soul has a destiny, and this time here on Atlantis is mine and that of many others as well.

I realize why past Atlanteans felt these beautiful crystals should be preserved and stored. I know the doubts I felt then are coming across now. Even if the crystals would have been grabbed by one or another race and been scattered far and wide through regular pillaging, at least they would have been out. Perhaps if the crystals would have been out, people from other cultures would have focused more on creating cooperative societies. I should focus on the present and gear my personal meditations to these very thoughts. I want it to go well this time on Atlantis and have everyone win and get to experience the utopia that existed here back in the day.

I am sure that will be the focus of the meditations from here on out, but I am beginning to think that whatever we do is just a stopgap measure until some military or another tries to take over in advance of their government and then that government comes in and wants to start laying down the rules. I just don't know if I can stand for this pristine continent to be sullied in that way. I know we will have to set up some sort of cooperative, and I know that works if everyone is invested. It was working beautifully at Civic Center and at DIA. I feel if we don't do something things will revert back to the old way of doing things, and that is not the right way. It was not working then and it will not work now. Now is our opportunity to create harmony among all people on a neutral ground.

Beatrice gave me an idea when she mentioned she felt a large cache of crystals below where she was meditating. She described how she felt them and felt them tuning in to her when she was meditating. We should find one of the larger caches, she said, and then ask the general for a summit of peace there so we will finally know his intent here.

Maybe they really just want to do their own thing here as well, but I don't see how that will not involve a struggle for power at some point. I don't love the fact that there are seemingly conflicting interests being represented here, and at some point push is going to come to shove in the jockeying for power. We hopefully can circumvent that here on a new continent if we the people decide on no leadership here. It is all going to boil down to the regular people and the people serving in the militaries. They either will continue to follow orders or they will not, and I am sure it would very much depend on the order and who was giving it.

I don't feel as fearful about the outcome as I used to. After the dream of Atlantis and then levitating myself today, I have to acknowledge that reincarnation exists and I was on Atlantis at some point. With these crystals and working with this energy, I just know things are meant to work out for the best this time around because we are all ending up here at the same time right away.

I know the vote to sink the continent was put to each and every Atlantean and they agreed, and it took the focus of each of them to sink it. I helped make the decision, campaigned for it even, and then helped store everything and relocate people. I would have been on a different continent at the designated time and participated in the last mind link of the Atlanteans. Perhaps I was even a facilitator of the event, one of the stronger mind linkers that helped hold everyone together since we were all in different physical locations. The force was far greater than we anticipated since we had never done anything like that before and we caused a lot of unintentional damage to other continents and peoples. All of this left a big energy imprint, I believe, which has kept us tied to Earth to bring things back to the balance that might have once existed. I think the time has come and the energy is aligned for all of us to get it right this time. I was one of the ones who caused grief because I thought I was right and made the decision about what was right for many people and caused loss of life.

I think I have been a healer in many lives since, to try to right the wrong. Clearly there is something to my ability to work with all this energy right away. I certainly never believed in any ESP stuff until approximately two weeks ago, so I must have honed my skills in another culture at another time to be able to tune in like this and have the crystals recognize my energy. I do get the feeling they are recognizing my energy, and it is like my mind dances in joy when I think of all the crystals being back out and getting everyone tuned in.

With all those thoughts churning through my mind, I figure I should go to the military mess hall too and look for coffee and something better than freeze-dried food to eat. Might that be me wanting the government to take care of me? No, I think it is more that I am finally ready to get the read on what is going on with the military. I am going to have to play an active role instead of hanging on the sidelines trying to coach. I will have to follow the gut as to where I need to be and when, and hope that it involves South Park soon.

11:36 p.m.

I think we had everyone on the continent except the general and his group at the meditation this evening. Regular people and military people, all of ours and most of those from other countries as well, numbering in the hundreds. It was amazing, if a little more disjointed than our meditation this morning. I was surprised that our military were allowed to join us, or maybe they were ordered to participate. Who knows?

But I like to think it was driven by camaraderie and fellowship and wanting to participate in the meditation. I was not the only one that had gone directly to the U.S. military camps this afternoon. It was fun at their mess hall. There was a lot of fellowship, and they were excited to be there and be exploring a full-on new continent. They would be getting down to business such as surveying the next day. Like children drawn to the fence when a new neighbor moves in on the block, civilians and others eventually showed up to their camps to talk with them and find out where they had come from and if they knew what they were there to do. They did not know much, just that is was to be a long deployment. Many of them had volunteered to come over, news that cheered me greatly because I am beginning to recognize that souls such as me are drawn here for reasons they cannot fathom. I think they are fellow souls who made the decision to sink the continent, so they are also back to heal what happened then. I asked a few of them if they were tired of not knowing what the mission is going to be, but none of them cared because that is what you sign on for when you join the military. You don't question; you follow orders. They were all curious about the meditation and how that worked individually and also how we did it as a group, so they were excited to join us.

The entire time I was there I could feel the cross currents of their mind-link communication. They are as tuned in to one another as the rest of us but I don't think they have done any large group meditations with the idea of trying the mind link or trying to work with the energy for any specific purpose. They loved hearing the stories of Atlantis and seeing the crystals we had put in place and the ones we were carrying with us. I think they were just as eager as anyone else to see what they could do with them, so we could begin working with things such as the pallets.

I could see why we might have such a strong contingent. If the military learned how to work all the new technology right away, they could then hide it away again. I think their commanders were told to let the personnel have a lot of free time to work with the crystals. Everyone wants to learn how to use them -- and use them to their best advantage if push comes to shove again.

Once Jon had shown the town hall format and it had been accepted by those gathered, we put it into effect right away to try to figure out how to get the water and lights going in the residence and gathering areas. The cache chambers seemed to have been lit from the inside, clearly powered by the crystals stored there, so we need to figure out which crystals power that sort of thing and how to get them to work. We arranged to get meditation areas set up near most of the crystals, but were also encouraged to meditate anytime, anywhere.

Then, and most importantly, we voted on the first big issue we face together here. What to do about the general. Everyone voted to track him down tomorrow and figure out what is going on with him. I hope we are not playing right into someone's hands here, but I cannot stand the thought of an ambush. I don't think anyone could pull that off without us sensing that they are coming at this point, but the issue does need resolution.

Tomorrow we do the sunrise meditation and then begin scouting for the general. Once we find him, we hope to send a small contingent of representatives from many countries to meet with him and his group. I am to be a part of the contingent.

The U.S. military are requisitioning buildings as they need them, and they are also going to be erecting even more camps all over the continent. They plan on mobilizing and getting set up even on the far reaches of those little keys. I suppose we are staking our claim early.

As usual, I think I will be the first back to the residence, and I am looking forward to my mind-reach for Mark tonight. I feel closer to him than ever. It is almost as if he expects me at a certain time now, and we meet up somehow. I am really hoping to get going on those crystals and be able to make a real connection with him to let him know I am alive and well and where I am. I just can't wait to see him again. It goes without saying that I feel the same way about the babies.

Day 13 4:14 a.m.

We were awakened at just after three this morning by the loud thunder of many large aircraft. What felt like a huge number of cargo planes flew in and landed around the amphitheater. The planes had Asian characters on their sides, but I could not tell from what country they came. We went out and sleepily greeted them with white flags waving. They waved us off, so we left them alone to get themselves set up. I was a little nervous because they did not seem overly friendly, but I was sure we would all manage.

It turned out they were not as interested in getting set up as they were intent on taking every single crystal and anything of value they could find to load up and fly off with. We had set the crystals in a fifty-mile radius, and they took every single one along with the planter things they were sitting in. My first instinct was to shout at them, or to run over and try to protect the crystals, but then I saw Leah walking with them and talking with them and actually helping them load things up. At first the military was not receptive to her at all, but Leah is Leah. She was moving among them and, I am sure, communicating with them verbally in their own language and telepathically as well. I could not understand what they were saying, but I did feel uncertainty and discomfort from them about what they were doing, which made them automatically defensive of those of us watching from the sidelines. Leah diffused that, and then Isolde, Ian and Consuela emerged from the darkness, each on a pallet heaped with goods and began helping them load up. By the end of the operation, the fifty-mile radius had been stripped bare and the new group had set up a camp near the amphitheater. They say they are going to remain heavily armed and do not seem welcoming or likely to attend the daily meditation. My worry is, what is going to happen when they want to strip Aladdin's Cave, which is being guarded by the general and his heavily armed force, and someone on one side or the other gets jittery and accidentally pulls a trigger?

I am glad we are going to try and meet with the general today, and if I am honest I am now seeing why we used to have military in place -- but I really don't want to be thinking like that.

It made me unreasonably angry that these outsiders felt they could come in and just grab anything and everything they wanted without asking, but I know this stuff is not mine to give. I could feel their discomfort at the grab, but by the end I could also feel that they thought their national interest had as much right to these things as ours does, and they are completely in the right about that. This is exactly the sort of thing I am supposed to be feeling welcoming of, but I hope our leaders don't try to rise to the occasion and think they have a right to protect this stuff. It is amazing how quickly this is going to play out this time around. I see more and more about why we are here and why we have already meditated with the crystals. I can feel my love built into the crystals as they fly off to who knows where. It is amazing to me that they got here so quickly after we broke out the crystals. It makes me realize that our government may not be the only country aware of what was buried out in the ocean and that there are plans in place or being formed all over the world for this continent.

I am also realizing more about what my unique standpoint brings this time around. I am not as attached to the crystals as I was back in the day, so it was easier to feel the feelings of anger when they were being stripped and then focus on letting them go. It is not as though they belong to anyone. In fact, they belong to everyone, and it is going to be best that we all bring them on line all over the world together. Whether another military is trying to get a leg up or trying to keep peace, it is important that all people are concentrating on the crystals and thinking about them as the energy from those thoughts pours into them and links them and focuses them. Crystals promote harmony and peace, and magnify those thoughts no matter where they are being stored.

I am going to head over to the military mess hall again. I am sure that is where everyone will gravitate. They have an endless supply of hot coffee going. I want to hear what they think of this new contingent or what they plan to do about it. I also want to make sure as many people as possible show up to the meditation in hopes we might get more rays of sunshine this morning.

9:45 a.m.

We are just getting ready to set out to parlay with the general. We had radio communication from him for the first time this morning, about an hour and a half after the meditation. We are meeting him and his group at one of the largest standing structures on the west side of the continent. It will be a smallish group going out to meet them. Military contingents from other countries will be there, but no representation of our U.S. military will be present. It was agreed there will be no weapons. Everyone will be flying their own planes there, and a fragmented part of our original group will fly over in the trusty cargo plane.

I understand they are a large group, and I am glad to be meeting them out in the open. I want to know what they have been doing all this time. I know what they have been doing physically, training and preparing, which has really strengthened their mind connection. I think they are the only group besides ours that has made an effort to work together and build a group energy that is unique to a group.

The meditation was jagged this morning as a result of all this military action, and we were only able to get puny rays of sun. I think that further shook us. Everyone was on edge about the crystals being taken, and we were having a hard time focusing -- myself included, if I admit it. I know those crystals were not mine, but to see them loaded up and taken without a word brought up a lot of deep emotions that I think were attached to the time long ago when perhaps this would have been the outcome if the

190

continent would not have been sunk.

To think; the more we pull from the caches, the more planes will arrive and take them. I am trying to maintain indifference. As Isolde said at the meditation, the crystals belong to no one. Of course we will continue to bring them out and it is just fine if every last one of them leaves the continent. We will make more. She was laughing as she told the group this, as if she were explaining to toddlers that of course they would someday grow out of that very favorite toy they could now not let out of their sight. She was trying to get the message through that the crystals are a conduit. They magnify the energy, but the energy comes from within and then connects and that you don't need the crystals to be in front of you. We are going to continue to find and bring up as many as we can and continue to learn how to work with them.

Leah disappeared over the horizon right after the meditation with a group of people who want to explore a little more of the continent and begin planting seeds and herbs. One of those people was Bea, of course, but Jon and Philip went along as well, which makes me feel unsteady. I knew our group would be going our separate ways; I just did not want it to happen before everything was tidily wrapped up with the general because if I had to face him I wanted to be with the entire group. It is doubtful they will attend the parlay. They left right after the meditation and before the radio contact with the general. I am sure they will see a stirring and the planes flying over, but they would probably ignore that. When they are with Leah, everyone is fully focused on her and not mind-linking to anyone else, and it is hard to know if Leah would be interested enough in a parlay like this to mention it to the others. I get the feeling she would not. She is not overly interested in affairs of state.

The regular military here on Atlantis, including the highest ranking, were beginning to be swayed to the idea of cooperative vs leadership, and then the rogue military landed last night and made the grab and now we are meeting with the general and it feels like they snapped out of our group energy and back into their military thinking. Now that the general has made contact, I can feel things fraying around the edges. If we become fearful of one another things could devolve quickly from there. One stray bullet fired here could start something ignorant, and I feel we must steer things in the opposite direction.

I feel that only Reginald and I in our group seem to see the gravity of this parlay with the general. Leah, Beatrice, Jon and Philip left after the meditation and before they even knew if we would track the general down today. Ian also left right after the meditation without saying anything to anyone as always, but I know I can at least count on him, Isolde and Consuela to be at the parlay since they are monitoring communication on the radios and know we have made contact with the general and he has agreed to meet. They do seem to be detaching a bit from the group as they go about their exploration further afield, but they know the general -- and this seems to be what Ian has been wanting since the beginning, so it should go smoothly.

I am glad to be getting everyone and everything finally out in the open so we can start getting more regular people to this continent if we can just convince everyone here to cooperate. The energy here has to be felt to be believed, and I know that will permeate everything today. We certainly were feeling heightened energy almost immediately after the geomagnetic stuff started going on, and now that we are standing at what may be the hub of the new energy it feels almost real enough to see.

I find myself somewhat nervous as we set out, even though this should feel like just another leg on this somewhat surreal adventure. I don't feel any malice from their group. I feel organization and purpose when I tune in with them. It is the purpose part that is making me nervous, I suppose.

7:22 p.m.

I thought my capacity for surprises was full. I seem to write a variation of that sentence every time I begin a journal entry.

We met with the general and his very large force this afternoon. We flew low over the continent for almost two hours to what I now think of as the convocation hall. I can see why the general chose that location for the meeting. Clearly it had been one of the central gathering places for the population, because it is an immense building. For such a huge building it has the most incredible acoustics. Ian, Reginald, Consuela, Isolde and I were some of the first to arrive in the cargo plane and went up the rise and into the building. The rise is the size of four football fields and the building itself is the size of one football field. When we walked in we saw that crystals of every color and shape had been placed in the alcoves and niches of the building. In addition, hundreds of the free standing crystal pillars of varied colors were planted in their intricately worked stands and scattered throughout the huge hall, like trees in a forest. The scene was dazzling even without sunlight. I could not figure out if the crystals had been in place the entire time or if the general and his group had set them in place. Being in the hall with the beautiful display settled my nerves, and as other people began to arrive and wander around and mingle, I almost forgot why I was there.

When the general and his militia came, they came on foot and their numbers were staggering. I could not feel an ounce of bad energy coming from a single one of them, but the visual of such a large number of what looked like an army coming forth so quietly up the rise caused a primal fear to surge and make me want to run. I wasn't the only one that felt a little uncomfortable. Our contingent, which suddenly felt very small, clustered close at the entrance of the building to watch the final approach. I felt Reginald's mind reach out and we mind-linked, and that was very comforting. Then he came to stand next to me and I felt immediately reassured and calmer. Then I looked around for Ian and Isolde and Consuela, and they were nowhere to be seen.

The general was different than I had pictured. For some reason I had an image of him as an older guy with gray hair. Instead he is a youngish, vigorous man who must have won his honors in the most recent wars. His charisma is almost as strong as Ian's and only stops short because the general seems so much more serious than Ian, more serious even than Reginald. I could not read their group mind link at all as they came toward us. It was as if they knew we would be reaching out and could block us with what I would describe as dead air space. They came in through the front entrance and enveloped our small crowd. The general seemed to be looking around for someone and eventually rested his gaze on Reginald, who happened to be the tallest and most commanding presence. The general looked at Reginald for a moment and then locked hard on him. "Nice to finally meet you, Reginald," he said. "Thank you for your persistence." He then asked about Ian, Isolde and Consuela and Reginald told him they flew here with us and have since disappeared. A brief smile escaped the general at this information.

He surveyed the rest of our group, and the quiet was almost palpable. I could not read him or mind-link with him, but I could see that his aura was peaceful.

"You think it is us who have come to fight and take ownership of this continent," the general said, "and that might have been true to a certain point. As you are going to see in a few minutes, you are going to have to make a decision about whether it is me or the U.S. government you will need to be facing off with. Before their representatives get here, let me give you the brief history of my involvement with Atlantis and the reasons I am here. Then, I am going to ask that you join forces with me. Hear my story and then make your call".

'The U.S. realized long ago, when instrumentation was becoming more cutting-edge, that there was something off the eastern coast of the United States that was putting out a great deal of energy, something that seemed like it could be a great power source. Radar and new equipment on ships and planes were beginning to detect odd, off-the-charts energy readings, but the technology did not exist to test how powerful the energy might be or to be able to send anything far enough down to test what it was or why it was beginning to show up on the more sophisticated instrumentation. The government and military put a small unit in place to do further research, and the unit was out doing just that off the coast of Florida one afternoon in a submarine when they got caught in a sudden, fierce storm. When the storm had blown its fury, the water was eerily calm and the submarine and crew found themselves drifting along with no engine, floating over the top of a structure that very much resembled a flat-topped pyramid. Their instruments were haywire, they could not steer, the sub seemed to be drifting along on a current and floated over two other pyramids. There was a light in and around the water, and the structures could clearly be seen. As they drifted over the third pyramid like structure, they could see through the clear aquamarine square that comprised the top into the chamber below, which was lit from within. The chamber had a replica of a large tree worked in silver and gold metal standing in the middle. The sculpture of the tree was a thing of indescribable beauty, they said. The leaves of the tree were made of thinly carved, multi- colored crystals that glittered and twinkled. It was almost as if the leaves fluttered in a light wind. The energy of the tree and the play of the crystals were such that they felt the tree was interacting with them. The chamber had alcoves decorated with multicolored crystals in every size, shape and color. The crew reported that as they drifted over and peered in, the crystals in the sculpture and in the alcoves seemed to brighten as they recognized energy being directed at them as the crew floated by. That same day, several airline pilots reported seeing the water all lit up and what looked like the tops of buildings just under the water, and fishermen in the area reported that the dolphins were going crazy, jumping and leaping out of the water, like they were dancing on the waves.

"The submarine had started out off the coast of Florida, and after floating for what felt like two hours, ended up near the Berry Islands in the Bahamas, where their engine started up and ran normally. None of their instrumentation, watches or cameras worked, so there was no documentation of the experience. They had their common experience and the corroboration of the story, which never varied. They were highly respected personnel, and their experience was the proof the U.S. government needed to dedicate more money and manpower to the project they dubbed the "Lost City." There were secret missions of very elite divers around the lost city area, and they found enough in the way of crystal relics to convince them that below the waters off the coast of Florida, and extending out past the Bahamas, lay the ruins of a civilization that had been highly developed. They were only able to get their hands on the smallest of relics, and then people began disappearing during the searches until finally they had lost so many people they had to call off the exploration in those areas".

"When scientists began working with the crystal relics that had been recovered, they noticed that certain people got better results when they handled them. Those people could see pictures inside or written words they could sometimes decipher. If three or more of the super-sensitive were gathered with the relic, the energy generated by the crystal could be measured -- or, more often than not -- went off the meter. The people who had the heightened sensitivity reported feeling changed after an experimental crystal energy charging, and where they had initially been attuned and empathetic they became what they described as psychic."

The government began testing certain higher-ranking leaders they thought might have abilities with the crystal relics, and the general said he happened to be one of them. He had a very strong affinity, the strongest seen yet, and once he got done working those pesky wars and winning honors he was recruited to lead the special unit that dealt exclusively with the lost city and the relics that had come from the lost civilization. His mission was to try to develop a link or learn how to work with the relics to build the great energy underwater in hopes that it could be eventually manipulated by the crystal relics. They were at this time also using drone subs to explore deeper underwater and using sophisticated instrumentation to gather data after violent storms, which seemed to presage the sightings and activity.

Until the general thought to try something new and different, they might not have gotten any further. He gathered the most talented from all past units under the pretense of wanting to test them to see if their abilities had lasted. When he got them together, he had them do some group exercises to get the relics revved up and then when he felt that energy come into the relics, he had the group shift focus to that underground city and think of the great power source there. He felt he had linked the relics to the great power source and indeed those exercises generated over a hundred reports from people in boats, divers close to shore, and pilots of seeing an underwater city lit up off the coast of Florida. Fishermen repeated the same stories of the dolphins dancing on the waves. The people who participated in those sessions reported feeling a great power in the lost city that helps unite the crystals yet never seemed eager to exploit the energy further and would not participate in further groups. In running the experiments, the general's psychic ability was sharpening to a fine point and he began to be able to facilitate groups of regular military and help them link energy. He began to experiment with group dynamics and facilitate larger and larger groups and get better and better results from the crystal relics.

In this way, the general found his way to the Hall of Crystal in his dreams. The Hall cannot be described with mere words, he said. The Hall began as a huge vein of quartz crystal that had initially been carved into a giant tunnel by the indigenous people. As the Atlantean culture grew spiritually, the Hall had grown and been added to by generations. It stood fourteen feet high and ten feet across, and stretched for at least half a mile. Like all other public buildings and structures, the Hall was open to all twenty four hours a day. People walked through it and meditated near it. It was the beautiful showpiece of their culture as well as their touchstone crystal, the crystal that links all other crystals. A crystal will absorb love and energy and will grow in size and clarity, and the Hall of Crystal had grown to its amazing proportion and beauty as generations focused their energy and love upon it. It was a thing of great power but, like any crystal, only to those adept. It was powerful enough that anyone could walk through and have a life-changing experience. An adept, on the other hand, had soul-changing experiences and could journey to other lands and other times. The Hall was used for so much it was an integral part of life. It also stores all the records of Atlantis, all the secrets to their technology, how their society worked and how they got that society from Point A to Point Z. The general did not report this dream to his superiors, as he felt the focus would then be on finding the Hall no matter what.

After the dream of the Hall of Crystal, he was drawn to spots across the country that had caches of smaller crystals. At one of those caches, he met Leah and had a very interesting conversation about his past lives on Atlantis. It was a struggle for him to believe he had had past lives on Atlantis, but enough evidence had piled up at this point that it was hard to deny. Using the Hall of Crystal as his focus for meditation, he began to see his past lives and why he had chosen to come to this life and become a decorated general. In a past life, he had been one to help make the decision to sink Atlantis, had campaigned for it as a staunch supporter and had convinced others. It was his duty in this life to lead others safely back, he said, and to open the continent for any who wish to come.

He began to hear a stir in Washington when geologists alerted leaders to a staggering rate of increase in underwater earthquakes and let them know that, combined with the frequency of recent continental earthquakes drawn against timelines on a simple graph indicated that something major would be occurring on the planet, and soon. As part of the high-level military, the general was part of the plans the elected government began putting in place for major disaster. It was then he noticed there did not seem to be much happening to secure the general populace, although he felt the technology was certainly in place to do so. He had some great ideas about how the world could be informed and shared them with his superiors. He got the indication that if he wanted to be safe he should fall into line and command his troops, and if he did fall into line he would be happy with the outcome. Knowing about past lives at this point, the general began to press his point and was ostracized by elected leadership and most of his fellow commanding officers. With little time, and seeing how things were going to go, he realized he was going to have to take his own route and stand up this time in a different way. He tried to speak up through whatever channels became available. Those channels included trusted associates, past special-ops groups he had facilitated, and at the very end, this militia group, which was eager to join forces with a high-level general.

It was at this point in the story that he let us know that representatives of the U.S. government were going to be landing soon to arrest him as a traitor to his government, and he reminded us we had a decision to make. They want him and his force out of the way, he said, because the U.S. plans on taking Atlantis as its own. In fact, the elected representatives plan on cordoning it off to other countries and calling it a U.S. military base.

The grand plan is to make the world a democracy. The leaders will say they are bringing democracy to the world, which is a grand idea and accepted by our military as their collective goal. The fact of the matter, he said, is that they are forcing their structure on other countries that may or may not want democracy. This is an outdated way of doing things and is going to risk violence. It will certainly put a hold on worldwide peace moving forward.

The representatives underground, calling the shots, believe they have the collective's interest in mind, and they also believe this is the correct way to proceed, to use military force to further push for worldwide democracy.

The general asked that everyone mind-link with his group when the military approached to help him convince them to react as people instead of a military force and to lay down their arms and declare peace. No one wants to be governed by fear or dominance, and the general promised he had a plan or two to move peace forward if we could believe in him right now and back him. He was not going to resist arrest, and he did not want any one of us to physically act either. If the plan did not work and it came to that he wanted to surrender peacefully.

Even as he was speaking his final words, we heard the military planes in the background and it seemed as if the entire force the U.S. military had brought landed at once on the outskirts of the rise. As they approached, I could see they were fully armed but the collective energy felt all wrong. It felt disjointed. It felt like many in the ranks disagreed with what was happening. They surrounded the rise and began to move forward, and I was beginning to feel a heavy despair, when I felt Reginald's huge hand envelop my own and our minds connect. His energy reminded me to connect to my center and hold peace.

At first there was noise and murmuring among the general's group as the military moved forward through the crowd. Then all was silent and the general's voice rolled out over the crowd, asking the military people to lay down their arms and declare peace. The military did not even pause in the move forward, and I felt Reginald's mind stirring. He and the general mind-linked and then he reached out and linked with the general's group. Their group energy had a deep belief and stillness about it. I reached out for the rest of our small group -- Isolde and Ian and Philip and Jon and Consuela – sending a signal that they needed to join in the mind-link for peace. I felt everyone on board, and then we all reached for Leah and her energy joined us like a silvery chime of laughter.

As a group we were led by the general to mentally encircle the oncoming army with love. The general and Reginald began sending a strong image to them of stopping the advance and laying down their arms. The military mind-link was strong as well, however, rooted in devotion to country and belief that theirs was the true course of action and they determinedly advanced.

They had us fully surrounded when two high-ranking officers stepped forward and asked the general to please come with them. He moved forward to do so, and I don't know where this came from or how it happened, but it was my voice that wavered out "Stop."

I wish my voice would have rung bold and brave like

Isolde's when she stepped forward way back when at Civic, but that spoken word had the effect of breaking the locked, focused energy each group had. It gave Reginald and the general the chance to link one more time and dial in together to what I would describe as the military channel. I always talk about the medical channel I connect with, and I would describe this as a frequency all military was presently tuned in to. I could feel Reginald and the general telepathically broadcasting the message and picture through this channel to the gathered military to lay down arms. Their combined force was so strong and passionate it was almost physically vibrating between them. I began to get the feeling the resolve of the military was crumbling and that they might be persuaded to lay down arms.

Sure enough, at that moment and almost in sync, the entire military force of the U.S. bent down and laid their weapons at their feet. It was a beautiful moment, and I felt love surging through the heart of every single person gathered there.

After that, everyone was kind of looking around, not knowing how to proceed, when Reginald's incredible baritone burst into song, the "Battle Hymn of the Republic," and everyone joined in.

"Mine eyes have seen the glory of the coming of the Lord."

"He is trampling out the vintage where the grapes of wrath are stored."

"He hath loosed the fateful lightning of His terrible swift sword."

"His truth is marching on."

The chorus swelled with every voice,

"Glory glory hallelujah."

"Glory glory hallelujah."

"Glory glory hallelujah."

"His truth is marching on."

Reginald then spoke.

"Freedom is the right of every soul. Let us join together and vow to keep this peace. Let us never raise arms against one another nor try to overpower one another. The time has come to join together and grant one another the freedom of peace on this new continent and around the world. I don't want to be a leader of anything, but I will give my time and my energy unfailingly to bring peace about."

He then lifted my hand in a gesture of victory. The action snapped me into the moment, and as I looked around at the very serious faces around me a little giggle escaped. It was more nervous reaction than anything, but after the giggle the serious looks turned downright comical and it spurred me to an uncontrolled fit of giggles. The laughter reverberated off the walls and because laughter is infectious, soon everyone was laughing and we all enjoyed a huge belly laugh. I must say, it was quite a tension breaker.

After that, people were splitting into groups to chat and some were beginning to scatter toward their transportation. Reginald and the general were deep in conversation when I realized I was going to have to beg a ride from someone if I wanted to leave any time soon. Our cargo plane was there, but there was still no sign of Ian, Isolde or Consuela. I kept looking around trying to figure out what I was going to do, and spied the burly guy from Civic Center. I was able to see him now as a brother instead of a menacing figure and decided, for that reason, to approach him. Our eyes met and I tried to reach out and mind-link to his energy first and realized why I had not been able to tap it before. When my mind reached out, he felt it and was able to still his mind enough that I could not get a read on him. I could not believe his energy had advanced to this elevated calm in the short span of time he had been on Atlantis. I smiled and walked over to him and we had a nice conversation.

This gave me further hope that this new peace is going to work. He said he had signed on initially with the general to further his own purpose and agenda, and then slowly learned what the mission on Atlantis was really about. That he would not be using his weapons and brawn on Atlantis and he and the rest of the group would have to learn to use their mind and the energy they would develop instead. He said he was not happy at first to have been so manipulated, but in working with the general he came to realize that the general was right and that the true power was in controlling one's own emotions and person, not trying to control others. He mentioned that he and the group had met Leah right after they arrived on Atlantis, and she had given them the same history of Atlantis and showed them the crystal tablets and other crystals and had answered questions. From there, they were on board with the general's true mission of bringing peace to the new continent.

Facilitated by the general, they had been to several crystal caches to get all kinds of crystals and have since learned how to tune in with them. One of the largest they had found was fifty feet tall and six feet around. Just as we had, to reach these rooms where the crystals are stored every person who wanted to enter had to touch the door before it swung open. It was the general's group who had put all the crystals in place in this convocation hall.

I wanted to talk with him further as our conversation had been so interesting, but out of the corner of my eye I could see Ian, Consuela and Isolde striding toward the cargo plane from the opposite direction of the entrance to the convocation hall, laughing with heads together as though they hadn't just missed a momentous happening. I could not figure out where they had come from, and for one split second I felt kind of mad at them for leaving me hanging. But then I laughed at myself for feeling like a child. I know I am not their responsibility and if they did not want to attend the parlay that was their choice. I knew everything had worked out exactly as it was supposed to, has always worked out exactly as it is supposed to, and will always work out exactly as it is supposed to. I have been lucky enough to be barely hanging on for the ride, and everything had resolved itself nicely.

I headed toward the cargo plane and loaded up with several other people. After a little bit, we headed back to the residence where I grabbed my notebook and began to try to document every detail exactly as it happened. I was writing and writing and needed to rest my hand and eyes, and I laid my head back and must have dozed off or gone into a hypnagogic state.

I looked around and realized I was standing at the entrance to the Hall of Crystal. Its clarity and form were as crystalline and as sparklingly beautiful as any diamond I had ever seen. The excitement I felt was as childlike as if I had ended up at a magic castle and found the door wide open. I could not wait to get inside. I stepped in, and there was Mark, gazing intently at an image superimposed on the wall. I was so thrilled that now he was here and we got to go in together I could barely contain my excitement, and as he turned to me I could read matching excitement in his face. Then I caught a glimpse of the superimposed picture. It was a picture of me writing this entry in this journal just before I laid my head back to rest my eyes.

That was too much, and I snapped back to where I was, resting with my head against the wall, writing the entry. In that moment I realized I was somehow there and here at the same time, and that time does not exist. There was also something in that moment that made me realize there is so much I don't understand yet and so much learning we need to be getting to. I must stop thinking and writing, shut the journal and get outside.

I loved seeing Mark and the Hall of Crystal. I think that image was precognitive. I think Mark and I will soon be exploring Atlantis together with our family and I am excited that we get to be a part of this new frontier. I am headed out to be with my fellow journeyers. It is going to be a great meditation and sing-along tonight.

The air is permeated by a relaxed, jubilant energy. Everyone is at ease and is coming and going and gathering in groups and chatting. It reminds me a little of the aftermath of the first town hall at DIA, except the energy is more free-flowing because everyone is completely open and everyone feels safe. We have even been able to recruit the new people from the planes last night, and they have agreed to also lay down weapons and strive for peace.

The amazing thing about the energy here it is that it is so very real. The term "walking on air" could be a real possibility for many. The energy is interactive, and I am looking so forward to seeing what we can build together in a short amount of time and then get to uncovering all the other learning out there.

The scientist in me is straining forward in excitement at the new discoveries, and the person in me is excited to know I will be seeing my family sooner rather than later.

Day 14 8:44 a.m.

A sunrise meditation with full sun -- a wondrous thing, I must admit.

The gang was all here for the morning meditation. Leah and Isolde and Ian and Consuela and Philip and Jon and Beatrice and myself and Reginald and people from every camp we have been to were represented. It seems anyone and everyone who has meant anything to me on this journey was there at the amphitheater.

Led by Leah and Isolde together, the meditation soared and the sun broke through strongly, shining down on us with radiance and heat.

When pressed, Leah finally told us how we would reach the Hall of Crystal. She reminded us of how the crystals are stored behind a door that has to be touched by everyone who wants to enter the storage room. She says that the very material the doors are made of is organic, and linked to the crystals inside and can read intent. There has to be no malicious intent on any single mind about to enter or the door would detect this and would not open.

The Hall of Crystal is protected in such a way but on a far greater scale. It was secured by the adepts of Atlantis and is hidden in a place and time that may or may not be our own. When every single heart in the world is aligned in peace, the alignment will trigger the solution to a mathematical formula that will translate to a beautiful melody that will play across all the dimensions of time, and the Hall will come back on line and into view and be accessible again to one and all.

Until we can reach the Hall of Crystal, we can uncover any and all of the crystals and make new ones and continue to focus on the Hall as a touchstone. Touch it with your mind, Leah said, and it interacts and makes the other crystals around you vibrate at a higher level. All is about love and cooperation, whether it is crystals, animals, people or planets. Cooperation and love are part of the universal law and the key to moving society forward quickly.

It should not be difficult to convince other cultures that the fabled continent of Atlantis has risen. Word will spread about the development's here, and surely people will come in droves to the new continent where they can find true freedom and peace.

As for me, I am going to revel in what happened here and the part I played in it. Tomorrow I will think of packing the backpack once more and trying to coordinate my flight home to South Park with Ian. Or perhaps Mark will prefer to bring the family here and meet me in Atlantis. If I have learned anything from this journey, it is that my capacity for surprise should extend to the infinite, and I am always exactly where I need to be.

So tonight I sing louder -- and maybe, just maybe, get up and dance.

The End

Made in the USA
Middletown, DE
16 December 2022

18783039R00119